W9-BYZ-748

The Gift of Family

Also by Mary Monroe

The Neighbors Series
One House Over
Over the Fence
Across the Way

The Lonely Heart, Deadly Heart Series
Can You Keep a Secret?
Every Woman's Dream
Never Trust a Stranger
The Devil You Know

The God Series
God Don't Like Ugly
God Still Don't Like Ugly
God Don't Play
God Ain't Blind
God Ain't Through Yet
God Don't Make No Mistakes

The Mama Ruby Series
Mama Ruby
The Upper Room
Lost Daughters

Gonna Lay Down My Burdens
Red Light Wives
In Sheep's Clothing
Deliver Me from Evil
She Had It Coming
The Company We Keep
Family of Lies
Bad Blood
Remembrance
Right Beside You

"Nightmare in Paradise" in *Borrow Trouble*

Published by Kensington Publishing Corp.

The Gift of Family

MARY MONROE

KENSINGTON PUBLISHING CORP.
www.kensingtonbooks.com

DAFINA BOOKS are published by

Kensington Publishing Corp.
119 West 40th Street
New York, NY 10018

All Kensington titles, imprints, and distributed lines are available at special quantity discounts for bulk purchases for sales promotion, premiums, fund-raising, educational, or institutional use.

Special book excerpts or customized printings can also be created to fit specific needs. For details, write or phone the office of the Kensington Special Sales Manager: Attn. Special Sales Department. Kensington Publishing Corp., 119 West 40th Street, New York, NY 10018. Phone: 1-800-221-2647.

Library of Congress Card Catalogue Number: 2020937097

Dafina and the Dafina logo Reg. U.S. Pat. & TM Off.

ISBN-13: 978-1-4967-3061-9
ISBN-10: 1-4967-3061-5
First Kensington Hardcover Edition: October 2020

ISBN-13: 978-1-4967-3062-6 (ebook)
ISBN-10: 1-4967-3062-3 (ebook)

10 9 8 7 6 5 4 3 2 1

Printed in the United States of America

This book is dedicated to my readers.

ACKNOWLEDGMENTS

It is such an honor to be a member of the Kensington Books family.

Esi Sogah is an awesome editor! Thank you, Esi. Thanks to Steven Zacharius, Adam Zacharius, Vida Engstrand, Lauren Jernigan, Michelle Addo, Norma Perez-Hernandez, Robin E. Cook, Susie Russenberger, Darla Freeman, the wonderful crew in the sales department, and everyone else at Kensington for working so hard for me.

Thanks to Lauretta Pierce for maintaining my website.

Thanks to the fabulous book clubs, bookstores, libraries, my readers, and the magazine and radio interviewers for supporting me for so many years.

To my super literary agent and friend, Andrew Stuart, thank you for representing me with so much vigor.

Please continue to e-mail me at Authorauthor5409@aol.com and visit my website at www.Marymonroe.org. You can also communicate with me on Facebook at Facebook.com/MaryMonroe and Twitter @Mary Monroe Books.

Peace and Blessings,

Mary Monroe

CHAPTER 1

My husband, Eugene Johnson, was one of the most successful entertainment attorneys in the Los Angeles area. Some of his most famous clients had become his friends, so we frequently received invitations to parties, movie premieres, award shows, and sporting events. We occasionally hosted star-studded affairs in our home, so there was never a dull moment in my social life.

Tonight, we were attending a party at the Malibu home of one of his newest clients, Otis Lee Kirksey. He was better known as Brother O and was a gospel rapper, of all things. The party was to celebrate his first contract with a major label.

"It's going to be very casual, Rosemary. More like a come-as-you-are event. You don't have to get too dressed up this time, or wear any makeup," Eugene told me over breakfast this morning. "You can even wear what you have on now and leave those doodads in your hair." He tugged the sleeve of my well-worn blue terry cloth bathrobe and tapped one of the pink foam rollers I used to curl my thick black hair.

It was only seven a.m. I didn't open the nail salon I owned until ten a.m., so I had plenty of time to make myself presentable. "And how would having a dowdy wife make you look, counselor?" I smirked, shaking a finger in Eugene's face.

"Just kidding, baby. Even if you didn't have such big gorgeous brown eyes, juicy lips, and those dangerous curves, you'd still be the most beautiful woman I know," he said with a wink.

After more than fifteen years of marriage, my husband still gave me compliments on a regular basis. And I enjoyed it, especially when I was looking frumpy. He finished his coffee in one long, loud gulp, wiped his lips with his napkin, and abruptly stood up. "Sweetie, I'd love to spend more time with you, but duty calls. I'll be in court most of the morning. It's going to be a very busy day."

"Tell me about it. We've got clients scheduled back-to-back today from the time we open, until we close. It's going to be this way every day until after Christmas next month." I glanced at the wall clock above the stove. "What time are you coming home this evening?"

"I'm not sure. As soon as I figure it out, I'll let you know," he replied as he adjusted his favorite Steve Harvey brand necktie.

"What time does the party start?"

"I'm not sure about that either. I'll give you a call when I get that information too. Now you have a blessed day."

Choosing a name for my business had not been easy. When I discovered that all of the cute ones on the list I'd compiled had already been taken, I decided to go with something simple: Rosemary's Nail Salon. It was a plain name for an establishment located in the heart of a posh Beverly Hills strip mall that catered to high-end clientele, but I liked it. I had worked for the original owner—who had called the salon Nails Incorporated—for two years, until she retired and sold the business to me. All four of the other manicurists she'd employed worked for me now.

Business was so spectacular, I'd added two more workstations and hired the two new best friends I'd met at cosmetology school, Min-jee McCall and Genelle Porter. They were my backup managers. When one of us had to take off, Min-jee's younger sister, Yoki, helped out. She had her cosmetology license, but had not accepted a permanent full-time position yet. She preferred doing freelance work for the time being. Lucky for us, she was always available when we needed her.

I had an interesting job. Some of our clients were colorful, fun to interact with, big tippers, and easy to please. But we had a few who gave us a run for our money—like Mr. Yamaguchi, my ten a.m. appointment for today. He was a divorced, retired sumo wrestler originally from Tokyo, Japan. He had been coming to the salon for five years to get pedicures. Mr. Yamaguchi had had a very successful career, so he was not hard up for money. He lived in a posh penthouse and indulged himself with beautiful young women and exotic cuisine. But he neglected his huge flat feet for long periods of time. When he did come in, we had to soak his feet for twenty to thirty minutes in a vinegar and Epsom salt solution to soften the dead and ashy skin enough so it'd be easier to scrape off.

"Aw. That feels so good. You do spoil me," he giggled as I dried his feet with a fluffy white towel. "My dogs almost looked like hooves before you started working on them. But do you still have to use that thing?" he asked, wincing like a frightened baby when he spotted the box cutter I had to use to trim his thick, scaly toenails when he let them grow too long.

"I wouldn't, if you came in more often," I scolded. "From the looks of things today, this will probably take longer than usual."

"Well, just be careful. You almost nicked me the last time," he complained. Then he giggled some more.

"You just sit back and relax. Take a nap if you'd

like," I said gently. "How about a glass of Pepsi or some mineral water to help you relax?"

"A glass of sake would help me relax more."

"Now you know we don't serve alcohol here," I reminded.

"That's all right. I brought my own." He grinned. "Just get me a large glass."

Mr. Yamaguchi was quite tipsy by the time I finished his pedicure. I had to summon his driver to help him to his Town Car. It was close to eleven thirty a.m. by then, so I headed to the Ivy for lunch. Min-jee and Genelle didn't want to go out. They asked me to swing by Pink's Hot Dogs on my way back and pick up something for them.

As I cruised down Wilshire Boulevard after my lunch, I admired the Christmas decorations some of the businesses along the way had already displayed. I made a mental note to pick up in the next few days some new lights and more tinsel for the salon and for home. My festive mood ended when I approached the intersection of Wilshire and Fairfax Avenue. It was the same spot where Biggie Smalls had been assassinated.

I was not into rap music. But I'd read a lot about him and it sounded like he'd been a very nice guy. It saddened me when I heard he'd been killed. Since then, every time I passed this intersection, I felt a cold chill. This time it was so bad, I pulled my Lexus to the side of the street and stopped. I felt okay after a few moments and was just about to leave when my cell phone rang. I usually let calls go to voice mail when I was in my car. But something told me to answer this one now. When I saw the name on the caller ID, my chest immediately tightened. I'd been going to the same gynecologist for almost twenty years, and this was the first time he'd called me personally.

"Yes, Dr. Miller," I answered, holding my breath.

"Hello, Mrs. Johnson. How are you doing?" My doctor was a jovial man, so his serious tone surprised me and ratcheted up my concern even higher.

"I'm fine," I mumbled.

"I'm glad to hear that." Dr. Miller cleared his throat. What he said next made me gasp. "You need to come in and see me ASAP."

"Oh? Is it something serious?"

"Yes, it is. But it's not something I want to discuss over the telephone."

"I'll call you back and make an appointment as soon as I get home and check my calendar."

"I'm sorry. But whatever you have, you need to reschedule it and come to my office. As a matter of fact, if you're able to come in *now,* please do so. I had two cancelations today, so I have some free time until three p.m."

"It's that serious, huh? I guess I won't be having much fun at the party I was going to tonight." I forced myself to laugh. "I hope you can tell me this much—will I live to see Christmas this year?" I wanted to make light of the conversation by laughing again. But this time I couldn't because I was truly scared.

"You'll be around for a lot of years to come."

"That's a relief. I'm not too far away from your office. I'll be there shortly."

I didn't know what to think during the drive to the medical center. What could possibly be so important that my doctor wanted to tell me in person? I wondered. He'd assured me I wasn't dying, but I was still concerned. There was only one thing I could think of important enough to be so urgent: I was finally pregnant again. And Dr. Miller wanted to tell me in person.

Eugene and I had been together since I was eighteen and he was twenty-two. He'd proposed a year into our relationship. But I'd never wanted to get married at a very early age. I liked being single. He was okay with that and told me more than once, "I'm willing to wait as long as necessary, even if it means we'll have to be married in a nursing-home venue." His dry sense of humor, kindhearted nature, and patience were some of the qualities that had attracted me to him.

However, as time went on, the main reason I delayed our marriage was because I had to take care of Daddy when he got sick. I probably would have put off getting married even longer if he hadn't died of diabetes complications two months after I turned thirty. Eugene and I were married six months later.

We started working on having children right after we were married. I got pregnant two years later. Unfortunately, I miscarried in my first trimester. And then again four years later. We waited a few more years before I tried to get pregnant again. We started trying again when I was thirty-nine. And here I was, forty-five and still trying to get pregnant.

I couldn't tamp down the hope that I was finally pregnant again. But then, why had my doctor sounded so glum on the telephone?

CHAPTER 2

It was a typical November day in Southern California—bright and warm, with beautiful leaves in every shade of brown on the ground. People were going about their business as if they didn't have a care in the world. The farther I drove, the more businesses and people I saw gearing up for Christmas. That made my mood even cheerier. I felt warm all over when I noticed a young woman pushing a stroller that held a toddler who was dressed in a Santa Claus romper. The woman was so busy texting, she walked into the street against the light. I honked my horn and gave her a stern look. Her mouth dropped open and she quickly put her phone into her pocket.

I couldn't believe how careless some people were when it came to the safety of their children. I had waited so long to have a child, I promised myself that I wouldn't let him or her out of my sight for one minute.

Being a mother had always been one of my biggest

dreams. I'd doted on my only sibling, Leonard, until he died of pneumonia. He was four and a half years old at the time and I was ten. While he was still in diapers, I used to push him around in the same baby carriage I used for my dolls. When he passed, I'd compensated for his absence by making as many friends as I could, and I would whine until Mama added more dolls to my collection. But that had not filled the void.

I got even more elated just thinking about how ecstatic Eugene would be when I told him the good news. He was such a pushover when it came to kids, and it was going to be a challenge keeping him from spoiling our child. To be honest, I knew that I'd have a hard time not doing the same thing myself.

I floated into Dr. Miller's office exactly fifteen minutes after our telephone conversation. "Go right in," his nurse told me with a somber expression on her face. That, and the fact that she wasn't smiling and making small talk the way she usually did, put a damper on my mood.

I entered Dr. Miller's office with caution. He was seated at his desk, poring over a chart in his hand. When he saw me, he abruptly set it aside and stood up. "Thank you for coming at such short notice." He waved me to the seat in front of his desk. The smile on his beefy red face made me feel more at ease. Maybe his nurse was just having a bad day.

"I think I know why you asked me to come in," I chirped.

"Excuse me?" he asked with both eyebrows raised.

"I'm pregnant, aren't I?"

With the smile still on his face, he shook his head.

My heart skipped a beat and my stomach knotted up. "I'm not?" I whimpered. I suddenly felt light-headed and my apprehension returned.

"You're not pregnant," he said softly. "I am so sorry. I know how long you and your husband have been trying."

"Do I have . . . cancer?" The word left such a foul taste in my mouth, it felt like I was going to throw up. Cancer ran in my family. It had already claimed my mother, her grandmother, and two of my aunts. Each year, I got my routine checkups on time, and did everything else I could to stay healthy. But because of my family history, Dr. Miller had me come in every six months for a Pap test. So far, I'd been lucky. Or had I? I held my breath as I awaited his next response.

"No, it's not cancer. At least, not yet. But because of your family history, the fact that your periods started when you were only eleven, and you've never given birth, you're at high risk for endometrial cancer."

"What is that?"

"It's another word for uterine cancer. This type usually grows slowly, and forms in the lining of the uterus. With regular checkups, it's usually detected before it spreads. If left untreated, it can spread to the bladder, the rectum, fallopian tubes, ovaries, and other organs. I . . . I received the results of your recent Pap test this morning and I was alarmed."

Chills thundered from my face to the bottom of my feet. I couldn't believe how hoarse my voice sounded when I spoke again. "So am I. What does this all mean? If I don't have cancer yet, I must have some options, right?"

Dr. Miller nodded. "Unfortunately, the abnormal cells in your tissue are very aggressive. You could develop full-blown cancer in a matter of months. A complete hysterectomy is your only option."

The words hit me like a giant sledgehammer. If he had told me that I already had cancer, I could not have been more stunned and brokenhearted.

"After the surgery, if you stick to a healthy diet, get plenty of rest, exercise regularly, and avoid stress, you could still live an active and fulfilling life for a very long time."

I didn't know what to do. Words tumbled out of my mouth. "Are you absolutely sure about the results of my Pap test?"

Dr. Miller nodded. "I know this is not what you expected to hear, but I am sure. I had the tests run twice, and each time the results were the same. But you are, of course, welcome to get a second opinion."

I shook my head. The last thing I wanted was to

hear the same thing from another doctor. "Hysterectomy is major surgery. How long will it take for me to heal? When my mother had it done, she had to stay in the hospital a whole week. When she came home, she was confined to bed for two weeks and had to limit her movements for another two months. She couldn't even go to work or do much around the house. As you know, she died the following year anyway."

"Well, medicine has come a long way in the past few years. In your case, I predict two or three days in the hospital at the most, and six to eight weeks' recuperation time at home. I have a few patients who returned to their regular activities within four to six weeks."

"Will I have to stay in bed when I get home?"

"That's up to you. You certainly can't go to work. But as long as you don't overexert yourself, you can move about the house like you do now. However, I advise you to get someone else to take care of your regular household chores. The first couple of weeks, you'll be fairly weak. Something as innocuous as bathing yourself or taking a short walk could wear you out. You'll definitely need some assistance—a relative or a friend would be nice. But a home-care nurse would be even better. Typically, they have more patience. What's more important is that they have experience."

"I see. Well, this is not what I wanted to hear today," I said in a raspy tone. After staring off into space for a few moments, I went on. "When should I schedule the surgery? I feel fine now and I have plans to do a lot of things every week until after Christmas. Could I do it in January or later?"

"You could, but I strongly advise you not to put it off that long."

I gulped. "Then how soon?"

"I'm available next Friday, then not again until the middle of December."

"That's a week from tomorrow. That doesn't give me a lot of time to find a good home-care nurse."

"I realize that. And with this being the holiday season, a lot of folks in that profession may not be available for a variety of reasons. Therefore, the sooner you initiate it, the sooner you'll find a suitable person. There are some excellent providers in this area." Dr. Miller sucked in his breath and glanced at his watch. "Any questions?"

"Is there anything I shouldn't do before the surgery?"

"You can still do anything you want, but only in moderation. The surgery will weaken you, so you should conserve as much of your energy as possible. Now go home and try not to worry."

"Try not to worry"? I was already so worried I could barely think straight. I wondered what I had done to deserve such a grim fate.

There was no way I was going to a rapper's party tonight.

CHAPTER 3

I held myself together until I reached my car; then I dropped down into the driver's seat and cried like the baby I'd never have. I used at least a dozen of the tissues in the box I kept in my glove compartment. I didn't stop crying until my cell phone rang, about ten minutes later. I pulled my phone out of my purse and cringed when I saw Eugene's name on the caller ID. I was tempted to let his call go to voice mail, but I didn't. I knew that if I waited too long to get back to him, he'd keep calling until I answered.

"Ro, where are you? I called the salon and Genelle told me you went to lunch before noon. It's now a quarter past three. She said you were supposed to pick up some lunch for her and Min-jee on your way back. When two o'clock came and went, and you hadn't returned to work or responded to the several voice mails Genelle left you, she and Min-jee got worried. Genelle called me."

"Um . . . something came up."

"Apparently. Well, what 'came up'? Are you all right?"

"I'm fine now. I got a sudden headache a little while ago, so I decided to drive around for a while until I felt better." I never lied to Eugene, but I did embellish the truth from time to time. Dr. Miller's news *had* given me a headache.

"Where are you?"

"A few blocks from the CBS building. I'm feeling better now, but not well enough to go back to work. And I'm not going to take the freeway and get stuck in traffic. I'm going to take La Cienega home."

"If you're not feeling well enough to go back to work or take the freeway, maybe you shouldn't be driving at all. Do you want me to come pick you up?"

"No, I know how busy you are. It won't take long for me to get home from here."

"But you're closer to the salon. Why don't you go there and let Genelle or Min-jee drive you home? I'll arrange for someone to pick them up and take them back to the salon or wherever they want to go."

"I'm okay to drive, Eugene. Call the salon back and tell the girls I'm okay and I'll call them later. When I get home, I'll take some Advil and lie down."

"I don't know, Ro . . ."

"Eugene, please get back to work and don't worry about me," I said impatiently.

"All right, then. But you'd better give me a call the minute you get home," he ordered. "And don't leave a voice mail or a message with my secretary. If I'm in a meeting, have her pull me out so I can talk to you directly."

"Okay, sugar."

"By the way, Brother O's party starts at six this evening. I'm going to go there straight from my office. I'll text you the address and you can meet me there. Is that all right with you?"

"Sure," I replied halfheartedly.

I drove home in a daze. It took only fifteen minutes for me to get from Dr. Miller's office to our house in El Segundo, a few miles from LAX. Two years after we were married, we decided to move from our two-bedroom condo in West Hollywood to a Spanish Colonial on a quiet street lined with palm trees. We'd planned to have several children, so we hadn't looked at anything with less than four bedrooms. The one we settled on had five bedrooms, a three-car garage, huge front and back yards, and a pool. We had great neighbors and a low crime-rate, so we planned to live in this family-friendly vicinity for a very long time.

When I got inside and stumbled to the living room, I took a deep breath before I flopped down on the plush blue couch. I sat as stiff as a plank, looking around the room as though seeing it for the first time. We'd hired one of the most experienced interior decorators in town, but I'd added a few touches of my own. There was a Ming vase above the living-room fireplace. I had found it in Hong Kong, where we'd celebrated our fifth wedding anniversary. And since I was somewhat of a penny-pincher, I had picked up artwork and a few other unique odds and ends from flea markets and estate sales. Framed photos of some of the celebrities Eugene represented were displayed on walls in our living room and in several other places.

I rarely spent a lot of time alone. When I did, I liked to reminisce about my past. I'd experienced the usual ups and downs of a middle-class African-American girl growing up in the L.A. area with two hardworking, doting parents. I was glad I had so many happy memories to focus on—especially after what Dr. Miller had told me. I had replayed my first meeting with Eugene in my head so many times, I knew every word verbatim. It always lifted my spirits. And that was exactly what I needed right now.

I knew after two dates with Eugene that he was the man I wanted to spend the rest of my life with. We'd met at his brother's wedding reception, six months after I'd received my high school diploma. My parents, who had owned a catering service back then, had provided the food for the reception. Daddy had asked me to help out because one of his servers had called in sick that day.

After Eugene had replenished his plate three times, he returned to the serving table again. He was the only one in line, and by then, the food was all gone. But he wasn't interested in eating any more. "We haven't met. I'm Eugene," he said, puffing out his chest. "And you're the Bruners' daughter?" he asked, giving me a wink.

"Yes, I am," I said dryly. I didn't know what to think about a boy from an affluent family like his, who was brazen enough to come on to a caterer. I decided not to do anything, like smile or wink back, because I didn't want to encourage him. But from the anxious look on his face, I had a feeling I didn't have to.

"Your parents catered my cousin's wedding last year."

"Okay." I wondered where the conversation was going.

Eugene looked around the church's reception area and then back at me. "I need to speak to both your mother and father."

I narrowed my eyes and glared at him. "Oh? Was there a problem with the food?"

"No, nothing like that. I just wanted to commend them for doing such a great job this time too. Everything was off the chain, especially the mac and cheese. And I want to thank you for giving me such generous portions each time I came back for a refill. I'm going to spread the word about the service and the food." He leaned forward and whispered, "My mother is so pleased. She's already talking about having your folks cater my wedding."

"I'm sure my parents will be glad to hear that. When are you getting married?"

"I don't know yet. I'm not even engaged. When I get to that point, you'll be the first to know . . ."

I rolled my eyes. I had heard some lame lines, but this boy was so original, I couldn't help but like him. "Thank you. It was nice talking to you. But we're about to clean up and be on our way," I said.

He looked around the room again. "You like to watch movies?"

I nodded. "Every day."

"I like action movies. You can't go wrong with Denzel or Wesley Snipes, or Sylvester Stallone."

"Well, I prefer movies that don't have a lot of violence and unnecessary explicit sex."

"Me too!" he said quickly. "I especially like romantic comedies. Some of the ones folks call 'chick flicks,' or something like that. Have you seen *Sister Act 2: Back in the Habit* with Whoopi Goldberg?"

"No, I haven't seen it yet. But I'd like to." I exhaled and narrowed my eyes. "Are you trying to ask me for a date?"

"Yup."

"I already have a boyfriend. I don't think he would like me going out with other boys. You and I can be friends though."

"If that's all I can be right now, that's fine." He laughed.

The "boyfriend" I'd been seeing at the time had other girlfriends, so our relationship had no future. Three days later, I broke it off so that when Eugene called later that week, I went to the movies with him to see Whoopi Goldberg in *Sister Act 2: Back in the Habit.*

Eugene's father was a municipal judge, who had been on the bench for over thirty years. His mother was a veterinarian, so the Johnsons lived a very comfortable lifestyle. Eugene was taking a break from his studies at Stanford Law School, up north in Silicon Valley. He would be leaving in a couple of weeks so I spent as much time with him as I could.

My parents' catering business didn't make a lot of money. But we lived in a modest house in the L.A. suburb of Hawthorne, and we could afford to take a nice economy vacation once a year. But at the time, they had a lot of other financial obligations on their plate, so college was not in my immediate future, if at all. Daddy's mother was in a nursing home that he had to pay for, until she passed four years later. His father had died a few years earlier. Mama's parents had died before Daddy's. But she had folks back in her Georgia hometown that she sent money to every now and then.

My mother had had three miscarriages before she had me. And another one before she gave birth to my deceased brother. Because of those tragedies, she and Daddy had always been overprotective of me when I was growing up. Despite our limited income, they encouraged me to work hard in every area. There was no money for college, but I was determined to be a success at something. I took a job as a server at a steak house to earn money. I didn't make much, but since my folks didn't make me pay rent, I could afford to pay the tuition to attend a yearlong training program at a cosmetology school in Long Beach. I couldn't afford a car, and I had a problem taking a bus to get there and back.

Mama died when I was nineteen, a year after I'd met Eugene. Shortly after that, Daddy's health began to fail. He could still take care of himself fairly well, but I never left him alone for long periods of time.

While Eugene was studying at Stanford, I never went out with any other boys. One reason was because we talked on the telephone, two or three times a week, for hours at a time. With work and school, hanging out with my friends, and taking care of Daddy, I never had much time to date anybody else anyway. It was the same way when Eugene finished law school and spent the next three years in the army.

Immediately after his honorable discharge, he joined a firm in downtown L.A. Eugene had a knack for impressing people. Within a year, he had so many clients on his roster, he could barely keep up. But that didn't stop him from adding more. The following year, I used some of the money from Mama's life insurance and bought my nail salon.

Each day was better than the last for Eugene and me, until today. How in the world was I going to tell him that I'd never be able to give him the children he wanted so badly?

CHAPTER 4

I next went into the kitchen and flopped down at the table. I wanted to reminisce about more recent things now. But before I could organize my thoughts and recall my conversation with Dr. Miller, the landline on the wall rang. It was Eugene.

"How come you're not answering your cell phone?" he asked.

"It's in my purse in the living room. I didn't hear it ring."

"How are you feeling now?"

"Better."

"Good. You do sound much better. I sure don't want to miss the party tonight."

"Oh. Yeah. Eugene, do you mind going without me?"

He hesitated for a few moments. "I thought you were feeling okay now."

"I am. But not well enough to go to a party. Besides, you know I don't like rowdy rapper get-togethers that much anyway."

"Ro, Brother O is a *gospel* rapper, remember? He only drinks wine every now and then. He never uses profanity, or even associates with any 'rowdy' people—that I know of. He's married to Frankcina Cobb, the bestselling, award-winning children's-book author. They are anxious to meet you. Besides, there will only be a few other folks there, so I doubt if it will go for longer than a couple of hours."

"I know, and I am anxious to meet Brother O and his wife. Not tonight though. I want you to go to the party anyway. I just want to stay home and . . ." I couldn't finish my sentence.

Eugene let out a loud, heavy sigh and a long moment of silence followed. "Rosemary, what's really wrong? Is there something you're not telling me?"

There was no way I could tell him what was "wrong" over the telephone. Dr. Miller had insisted on telling me in person, and I felt the same way about how I'd tell Eugene. I chuckled and said, "You worry way too much. Go on to the party and have a good time."

I walked to the couch and stretched out and attempted to read the latest issue of *Newsweek*. I put it back on the coffee table within minutes, because I couldn't concentrate on any of the articles. At ten thirty p.m., just as I was about to doze off, I heard two vehicles enter our driveway. Before I could get up, the front door flew open and in walked Eugene. A couple I had never seen before was with him. I stood up immediately. Eugene strutted up to me and grabbed my hand.

"Ro, this is Brother O," he introduced. "The next big star on the horizon." Before I could respond, he went on. "And this is his wife, Frankcina." He put his arm around my shoulder and pulled me closer. "Folks, meet my wife, Rosemary."

"It's nice to meet you both," I muttered, shaking the rapper's hand and then his wife's. "I'm sorry I couldn't make it to the party." Brother O had short, spiky blond hair, an overbite, and he wore horn-rimmed glasses. He looked more like a moon-faced, nutty professor than a rapper. His wife reminded me more of a brown Barbie doll than a children's-book author. They appeared to be in their late thirties. I was glad I hadn't put on my nightgown. But I was certainly not in the mood to entertain guests, especially ones I was meeting for the first time.

"Call me Franny. Eugene has told us so much about you," Franny said with a grin. "I'll be checking out your nail salon soon. The one I've been going to for over ten years is going to be closing for good at the end of the year."

"Thank you. We'd love to have your business," I replied, grinning too. Despite the sadness that had overwhelmed me, I was still able to put on a happy face.

"I love this house," Brother O said, scanning the room. "It's so huge, it makes ours look like a shoe box." We all laughed.

"A 'shoe box' that happens to be on the beach in Malibu," Eugene pointed out.

"True. But it's not decorated as beautifully as this place," Franny said.

"We love it here. The day we moved in, I knew it was going to be the last place I'd ever live." Eugene spoke with his chest puffed out. "You folks have a seat, please." He waved them to the couch, and he plopped down into the love seat facing them and pulled me into his lap.

"Can I get anything for anybody?" I asked, smoothing down the sides of my skirt.

"No thanks. It's late and Eugene told us you're not feeling well, so we won't stay long," Franny said, looking apologetic.

"Oh, I'm okay now," I insisted. "You can stay as long as you'd like. How was the party?"

"It was great. One of my mentors from Mississippi is in town for a revival, so he joined us. I hadn't seen him since I moved to California three years ago, so seeing him was a treat for us. We'd love to stay and visit with you fine folks longer, but we have to get going soon. I wish we would have ended the party earlier and come right after we tucked the kids in," Brother O said, beaming like a high-wattage light-bulb.

"Oh. How many kids do you have?" I asked.

"Three," Franny said quickly, rolling her eyes. "We plan to have just one more."

"I keep telling Eugene he'd better get on the ball! Time ain't on your side, my man. Tick tock, tick tock," the rapper said, snapping his fingers and giving Eugene a mournful look.

"We still have a few good years left, so I'm not worried at all," Eugene responded with an anxious expression on his face. I was surprised to hear him say such a thing. We were both in our forties, so time was not on our side. "Besides, we wanted to make sure we'd be in the best financial shape possible before we started our family."

I sighed. We'd been in pretty good financial shape for at least the last ten years. This was the first time I'd heard Eugene offer such a flimsy excuse when somebody brought up the subject of children and the fact that we didn't have any yet. I had no idea if he'd told anybody, other than his brother, that we'd been trying to have children for years. I'd only told Minjee and Genelle.

"How old are your children?" I asked.

"Billy, the eldest, is seven. The girls, Lynette and Sandy, are five and four."

"That's a lot of work," I commented. "You both must have your hands full all the time."

"Tell me about it. Those three keep us on the go. Whoever said it takes a village to raise a child really hit the nail on the head. We'd be lost without our live-in nanny. And Franny's parents live in Long Beach. They like to keep the kids two or three weekends out of each month, and also when I go out on tour, so we still get to have a lot of time to ourselves," Brother O said.

"Being a parent can be chaotic, but I wouldn't change a thing. Family is what life is all about," Franny said with a wistful look in her eyes. If she hadn't changed the subject when she did, I would have. "Rosemary, Eugene tells us your business is booming."

Before I could respond, Eugene blurted out, "Oh, is it ever! Every time I drive past that place, the parking lot is full of luxury cars. And"—he paused and chuckled—"you wouldn't believe the antics of some of the patrons. Rosemary has told me stories about some of them that made me laugh until I cried." He turned to me and jabbed my side with his elbow. "What about that screenwriter's wife who threw a hissy fit because you wouldn't give her poodle a French pedicure?"

I laughed and shook my head. "She's really a nice woman if you get to know her. After the poodle incident, she stopped coming to us for a month. When she returned, she acted like nothing had ever happened."

Despite the fact that our guests had said they didn't plan on staying long, they didn't leave for another hour. When Eugene walked them to their Cadillac Escalade, they talked outside for another twenty minutes.

"Whew. I thought they'd never leave," Eugene complained as he trotted back into the house, shaking his head. "If I'd known they were going to be so long-winded, I wouldn't have invited them over."

I blew out a loud breath and wrung my hands. "Eugene, sit down. We need to talk."

He gave me a puzzled look as he flopped down next to me on the couch. "What about?"

"I didn't tell you everything when you called me this afternoon," I started, then abruptly stopped.

There was a frantic look on Eugene's face. He reared back and narrowed his eyes. "Don't stop and leave me hanging. What did you *not* tell me?"

"After I had lunch, Dr. Miller called me up on my cell phone and told me to come to his office immediately."

"Oh?" There was a frightened look on his face now. "What did he need to see you about?"

I cleared my throat and took a deep breath. "There was a problem with my Pap test—something that could lead to cancer. I don't need to go into all the details, but, according to Dr. Miller, if I want to lead a healthy and long life, my only option is a complete hysterectomy. That means—"

"I know what it means," he said sharply.

I said it anyway: "We'll never be able to have children of our own. I am so sorry." I couldn't believe what I said next. "If you want to divorce me, I won't contest it."

CHAPTER 5

If I had pulled a knife on Eugene, he couldn't have looked any more frightened. He gulped so hard, his eyes crossed. "'Divorce'? Do you want a *divorce*? Is that what this is really about, Rosemary?"

"I know you want children, and if I can't give them to you, maybe you'd rather be with someone who can."

"If *you* want a divorce, you can forget it."

"I just wanted you to know that you have a way out," I whimpered.

Eugene reared back some more and spread his arms. "A way out of what?"

"You want a family."

"I already have one!"

"You want a family with children. I want the same thing," I mumbled.

Eugene held his hand up in the air. "Hold your horses. You're beginning to talk out of your head. We can still have a family with children. There are hundreds, thousands, of girls and boys out there who need homes."

I swallowed hard and shook my head. "I don't want to take in another foster child." Several years ago, we'd fostered a fourteen-year-old girl named Rhonda. She'd been neglected and abused by her birth mother, and eventually abandoned. During her time with us, she'd blossomed. When she turned eighteen, she reconnected with her birth father and decided to leave us and move in with him and his wife in Compton. Rhonda had only visited us once and called twice since she left. We had her telephone number and called regularly to see how she was getting along, until the phone number got disconnected. Eight months after her departure, we ran into her at a farmers' market. She was married to a marine, pregnant, and in the process of joining him where he was stationed in the Philippines. That was the last time we communicated with her.

The following year, we took in a sixteen-year-old boy named Dillon. He reconnected with his birth parents when he was nineteen. A month later, he went to live with them. Dillon kept in touch with us for a few months. But when his family moved to Texas, we never heard from him again. When the social worker we'd been working with offered to place another child with us, we'd declined.

"If you're talking about us taking in another foster

child now, you can forget it. Having children 'on loan' is okay for some folks, but not for me," I snapped. "I guess it's time for us to adopt, which is what we should have done a long time ago."

Eugene gazed at the wall for a few seconds and rubbed his forehead. When he returned his attention to me, he looked miserable. "Well, we don't have a choice now. The sooner, the better. Some adoption agencies consider couples over fifty too old. Especially if they want an infant or a very young child."

"We've still got some years before we reach fifty," I said, scooting closer to Eugene. I massaged his shoulder and that seemed to make him feel better. He didn't look so woeful now. "It would probably help if we lowered our expectations. I'd love to have an infant, or a toddler. But there are a lot of kids out there who are hard to place because they are older or have special needs. If we take in one of those, maybe we'd have better luck getting an infant later."

"I agree." Eugene blew out a loud breath and scratched the back of his neck. "Meanwhile, we need to focus on your upcoming surgery. Did Dr. Miller say when you should have the surgery done?"

"I wanted to put it off until after the holidays, but he advised me not to. He says the condition is so serious, even a few weeks' delay could have some severe consequences."

"My God," Eugene moaned.

"I'll be out of commission for several weeks. Six to

eight, Dr. Miller said. I'll be confined to bed for some of that time. I'll even need somebody to help me bathe and assist with all of my household chores. Maybe not for the whole time, but at least the first week or two."

Eugene shrugged. "I'll have to work from home until you recover."

"No, I don't want you to do that," I insisted, shaking my head so hard my neck ached.

Eugene draped his arm around my shoulder and squeezed it. "Ro, you just said you'd need help for a while. Everybody we know works, so what choice do we have?"

"We'll hire an in-home health-care worker. That's what my doctor suggested." I exhaled and blinked. I had been feeling miserable since this afternoon. Now I felt numb, confused, hopeless, and even more miserable. "I wish this had come up after the holidays. I was looking forward to celebrating Christmas with your brother and his family."

Eugene's older brother, Lawrence, was a bank president in Westport, Connecticut, where he lived with his wife, Lena, and their four teenage children.

"Pffftt!" Eugene gave me a dismissive wave. "Christmas is more than a month away. By the time it rolls around, you should be as fit as a fiddle."

"That may be true. But I won't be the same person."

Eugene squeezed my shoulder again. "Rosemary, you will always be the same person."

We remained silent for a few seconds. What I said

next caused a lump to form in my throat. "Now, when people ask us when we're going to have children, or why we don't already have some—"

"We'll just tell them the truth. It's not the end of the world, honey." Eugene sighed and checked his watch. "It's later than I thought. Let's go to bed. We'll discuss this more in the morning."

CHAPTER 6

When I went to bed, I only slept for about three hours. The way Eugene tossed and turned, he probably slept even less.

I got up at seven a.m. on Friday and made coffee. I wasn't surprised to see that Min-jee and Genelle had sent text messages and left voice mails. I wasn't ready to talk to them yet, but I didn't want to leave them in suspense any longer. I sent them the same text message: **Sorry I didn't come back to work or call yesterday. Something came up. Will explain everything when I get to work this morning.**

I was still in my bathrobe and on my second cup of coffee when Eugene entered the kitchen, already shaved and dressed in one of his favorite Armani suits. I stared at him, proud to have such a dapper husband. With his shaved head, full lips, and intense eyes, he resembled a pudgier, slightly darker version of actor Vin Diesel.

"You want bacon or ham with your eggs?" I asked.

"Don't bother. I'll grab something later," he said in a rushed tone. "I don't have much of an appetite right now anyway."

"Neither do I," I murmured.

Eugene gave me a hopeful look before he leaned down and kissed my forehead. "Baby, everything is going to be just fine."

"I know. I just never expected us to end up like this."

"End up like what? Rosemary, do you know how many other couples would love to be as blessed as we are?" Eugene didn't give me time to reply. "Unfortunately, we can't have everything we want. We'll never have children of our own, but think of all the ones who've been neglected, abused, or abandoned. They'll never have parents. Maybe our role in this unpredictable, mysterious scheme of life is to be the answer to some unfortunate children's prayers. If everything had worked out and we were able to have children of our own, there'd be two or three other children—however many we decide to adopt—who would never know the privileged life we can give them."

"I know all of that," I whimpered.

"Okay, then. Adoption is the best we can do now, Rosemary. Or do you want to consider hiring a surrogate?"

"I don't think so. I don't like some of the things I've heard about that."

"Like what?"

"I saw something on TV about a surrogate who decided to keep the child that a couple had paid her to carry for them. They took her to court and ended up letting her keep the baby. I know I wouldn't survive something like that. And if we couldn't keep a close eye on the surrogate during the pregnancy, who knows what she'd be putting into her body?"

"You make some good points," Eugene admitted. "Just don't spend too much time stewing about this."

"I won't. I agree that adoption is the best we can do now." I let out a loud breath and stood up. "I should probably stay home today."

"I have a couple of meetings this morning, but I could reschedule them and stay home with you."

"No, Eugene. I don't want you to do that. It'd probably be better for me if I go in. Being busy would keep my mind off . . . well, you know. The first chance I get this morning when I get to the salon, I'll contact one of those home health-care agencies. They can line up some candidates for me to interview. Dr. Miller said I'll need assistance for the first two or three weeks, but I'm going to request someone who can stay the whole eight weeks I'll be off work."

"I was going to suggest that myself. But why don't you let me deal with the agencies. I'll have them line up a few candidates. You and I can interview them together. If we're going to have a stranger in our house, I want to meet them face-to-face first."

"You already have enough on your plate. I don't

want you running back and forth from here to your office for something I can handle on my own. Don't you trust my judgment?"

"You know I do. All right. Have it your way. But I'll find some time to call an agency today myself."

"All right. Just make sure you tell them exactly what type of assistant I'll need."

"I will, sugar."

I arrived at my salon an hour earlier than usual. I was surprised to see Min-jee's shiny silver Range Rover already parked in her usual spot. Before I could even get out of my car, the employees' entrance back door flew open and Min-jee appeared in the doorway with her arms folded.

"You're a sight for sore eyes," she yelled as I slowly piled out and dragged my feet toward her.

I rarely took Friday off. It was usually our busiest day. A lot of bored housewives and obnoxious trust-funders dropped in to get a broken nail repaired or to change the color of polish they'd worn for only a day or two.

"Rosemary, what is going on with you?" Min-jee wrapped her arm around my waist and ushered me inside.

Instead of answering, I sniffled and started crying again.

"Oh, my God. Rosemary, what is the matter? Did something happen between you and Eugene?"

I shook my head and stumbled into the spacious office I shared with Min-jee and Genelle. In addition to two dark cherry-oak desks and several swivel chairs, we had two file cabinets and a watercooler, like the two we had outside in the main room. I plopped down in a chair behind one of the desks, and Min-jee stood in front of me, with her hands on her hips. "It's worse than that," I managed. I told her about Dr. Miller's phone call and my visit. The whole time she stared at me with a blank expression on her face.

When I stopped talking, she sucked in a deep, loud breath and told me, "A hysterectomy is not that serious. You know I had one two years ago and I'm doing just fine."

"You'd already had your kids," I said.

"Well, yes, but—"

"You don't have to tell me. I know Eugene and I can adopt. We've already discussed that, and we'll be looking into it in the very near future. I just never thought I'd have to let him down."

"Oh, please!" Min-jee hollered with a scowl on her face and her finger wagging at me. "If you think having to adopt a child is a 'letdown,' you need to think again."

Min-jee had been adopted when she was only eight months old. Her birth mother had abandoned her hours after her birth. A wealthy couple from Los Angeles, who would eventually adopt four more Korean orphans, had traveled to Seoul to rescue Min-jee from the run-down orphanage she'd been living in. She was one of the most well-adjusted people I knew, and one of my best friends for life.

"I hope I don't sound too harsh. I don't want to make you feel any worse than you already feel. Have you told Genelle yet?"

"No. I haven't spoken to her since I left for lunch yesterday. I sent her the same text I sent you this morning."

"I wish you had called us up yesterday so we wouldn't have spent so much time worrying about you. Why didn't you stay home today?"

"I didn't want to leave you guys in a lurch, like I did yesterday afternoon. Who took care of Mrs. Spaulding?"

"Who?"

"That fussy brunette who comes in every Thursday afternoon after her Zumba class and only allows me to do her nails."

"Oh, her!" Min-jee shook her head, rolled her eyes, and groaned. "She didn't show up. And she didn't even bother to call and cancel." Min-jee rubbed up and down my back. "You feel so tense."

"I am tense," I confirmed.

"Did your doctor set a date for the surgery yet?"

I nodded. "A week from today. I'll have to take off for a few weeks. He said six to eight. Do you think you can get your sister to fill in for me?"

"I hope so. She's been talking about going to Hawaii in the next couple of weeks, if she can find someone to go with her."

"Talk her into going *after* I return to work. And let her know that I'll pay her time and a half for whatever time she can cover for me."

"Honey, I'm sure she'll go for that. I don't think anybody can say no to you."

I gave Min-jee a thoughtful look. "Not even an adoption agency?"

"Honey, something tells me that you and Eugene are going to get more than you hoped for."

CHAPTER 7

When Genelle arrived fifteen minutes after me, I repeated everything to her that I'd shared with Min-jee. "I wish you had called one of us last night. I hate to think about you sitting in the house alone until Eugene got home."

"I wanted to, but I didn't want to discuss it with anybody else until I told Eugene."

"Who else have you told?"

"Nobody yet. It's not something I want to broadcast to too many people anyway. We'll tell family and maybe a few other close friends, but that's about it."

"Well, we are as close as family and I appreciate you telling us now."

"I feel the same way," Min-jee said with a nod.

We were an odd-looking trio. I was of average height and weight, attractive but not classically beautiful—no matter how many times Eugene told me that I looked as good as a couple of his clients who had graced a few glamour-magazine covers. Min-jee, with her cute, round baby face and size-two body, didn't look a day over thirty-five, but she was the oldest at forty-seven. Forty-four-year-old Genelle was a dead ringer for Queen Latifah, and was just as sassy. She had been a regular customer at the restaurant my late parents had owned before they'd started their catering business. She cooked and ate like it was going out of style. Somehow she managed to remain a size sixteen, three sizes larger than me.

The minute we opened for business, customers, with and without appointments, filed in like soldiers. We had two large flat-screen TVs; one faced the workstations and one was in our waiting area. We also provided a vending machine, a magazine rack, with the most recent gossip and fashion publications, two watercoolers, and a restroom to keep everybody happy. One evening I saw a TV news report about a woman who had attacked her manicurist because she'd given her a "mean look." Luckily, the worst I ever had to deal with was Mr. Yamaguchi's loathsome feet.

A lot of folks thought that because of our location, we didn't have to deal with petty concerns, like some of the low-end nail salons in the inner-city districts did. For instance, they thought we didn't have to interact with unsavory characters who got their nails done and then refused to pay. Truthfully, those types were everywhere.

Shortly before eleven a.m., a husky female TV producer strode in for her appointment. The last time she'd come in, she'd paid me with a bad check. Before she even flopped her fat frame into a seat, I let her know she had to pay in cash or with a credit card. She didn't like that one bit.

"Why? I'm a regular, and the last time I was here, you accepted a check," she said in a gruff tone.

"And the bank returned it unpaid," I informed her.

"Oh, my God! I . . . I forgot I closed that account last month! Why didn't you call me up and let me know?"

"I left you three voice mails, Mrs. Schultz."

She sucked on her teeth and gave me a sheepish look. "Tee-hee-hee," she giggled. "That must have been when my phone was on the blink and not recording voice mails. I am so sorry. It'll never happen again. Hold on. I'll write a check from a different bank." Mrs. Schultz rooted around in her Louis Vuitton purse for a few seconds. "Dohhh! I changed purses last night and forgot to transfer my checkbook." There was a frantic look on her face. "Don't move!" she ordered, holding her hand up to my face. "My bank is in the next block. I'll be right back!" she yelled as she sprinted out the door.

She returned twenty minutes later and pulled a huge wad of bills out of her purse. She covered last week's bad check and gave me a hundred-dollar tip for the "inconvenience." I immediately did her nails. Not only did she pay me double for a regular silk wrap, she gave me another hundred-dollar tip.

The agency that Eugene had contacted called me up a few minutes after three p.m. They were eager to accommodate me. They'd set up the first interview for Monday, and two for Tuesday. I hoped that I'd like the first person enough so I wouldn't have to conduct but one interview.

"If the interview does not go well on Monday, I'll probably have to take off Tuesday too," I informed Min-jee and Genelle.

"If you're going to have surgery a week from today, go home now and stay off until after you recover," Min-jee suggested. "I spoke to my sister a little while ago and she said she'd postpone her trip to Hawaii and fill in for you."

"Great. Tell her she can start Monday morning."

The first applicant was scheduled to meet with me Monday morning at nine o'clock. She showed up thirty minutes late. There was an embarrassed expression on her face when I opened the door.

"Sorry I'm late. It took me a while to find my bus pass." She gave me a weak smile as she sashayed into my living room. "I'm Julie Jennings, but you can call me Julie. The agency sent me."

"I'm Mrs. Johnson," I replied cordially, reaching out to shake her hand.

She was at least twenty-five, but was dressed more like a teenager, wearing a low-cut white blouse and a short plaid skirt underneath a tan trench coat. "You the sick lady that needs somebody to start working next Monday?"

Before I could answer, she added, "If you don't mind, I'll keep my coat on. It's kind of cold in here." She unbuttoned her coat and looked around.

"Yes, I am the lady who will require some home care for a few weeks," I said stiffly.

"Oh. I thought you'd be real old," Julie muttered as she flopped down on the couch. I remained standing with my arms folded. "The agency said your husband works with a lot of stars."

"He handles contracts and other legal issues for some entertainers," I stated.

"He work with any real big stars I would know? My cousin been trying to get a job on TV. He was on *Judge Judy* when he sued his mechanic, and he was a contestant on *The Price Is Right*, but that's as close as he's got to show business so far. Maybe your husband can help him get his foot in the door. He can act and sing real good. And people tell him all the time he looks a lot like Jamie Foxx."

It was hard for me to remain composed, but I managed. "If you don't mind, I'd like to discuss the position first," I said firmly. I sat down in the chair facing her.

"Okay, then," Julie said with a shrug.

"I may be completely confined to bed the first week or two. I won't be able to do much of anything during that time. I will need help getting in and out of bed, and bathing."

Julie nodded. "Well, I got a lot of experience. I was a nurse's aide in Chicago for two years before I moved out here last March."

"I see. There will be some light housekeeping and you'll need to prepare lunch for me, and maybe a midafternoon snack from time to time. My husband will take care of my breakfast and dinner. He leaves for work between nine and nine thirty a.m., so I'd like for you to be here before he leaves—at nine a.m., Monday through Friday. I'll expect you to stay until six p.m., which is when he normally returns home, give or take a few minutes. Some days he has to work late or spend time with clients, so I might ask you to work overtime, with not much notice. You will be paid time and a half when you stay past six."

There was such a blank look on Julie's face, it looked like she had turned to stone. "*Housekeeping? Cooking?* The agency didn't say anything about that. When they told me what your husband did, and that you own a nail salon in Beverly Hills, I assumed you had a maid to do the housekeeping and cooking. The last two ladies and an old man I took care of, they all had maids *and* butlers."

"Well, we don't have a maid or a butler. And my

husband told the agency the specific responsibilities the position would entail. Didn't they share that information with you?"

"Um, I think they did say something about preparing meals, but I don't remember them mentioning cleaning house, especially one this big." With a heavy sigh she added, "Oh, well. I guess I'll try it for a week or two. I won't be late when I come next Monday. I'll put my bus pass in my purse Sunday night, so I won't have to hunt for it like I did this time."

I stood up. "I'm sorry, but I have more candidates to interview before I make a decision," I replied.

"Oh. The agency said you needed to hire somebody right away, so I thought I was the only one they was sending." Julie looked so crestfallen, I felt sorry for her. But there was no way I was going to hire her. "I hope I hear from you. You seem like a nice lady."

"Thank you, Julie. You seem like a nice lady too. Now, you have a good rest of the day," I said in the most pleasant tone I could manage under the circumstances.

"You don't want the names and phone numbers of my references?" She stood up and started buttoning her coat.

"That won't be necessary," I said firmly. "Thank you for coming."

After she left, I dropped back down on the couch. I was disappointed, to say the least. I thought that anybody looking for work these days would go out of their way to make a better first impression than Julie Jennings had.

"It can't get any worse than this," I mumbled to myself.

I was wrong.

CHAPTER 8

The woman I was scheduled to interview on Tuesday arrived right on time and was appropriately dressed. She was in her fifties and had twenty-five years of experience. She seemed like a good prospect, until I smelled alcohol on her breath. Since she'd come by bus all the way from East L.A., I was polite enough to invite her in, even though she had no chance of working for me. But I gave her a cup of coffee and asked her a few general questions anyway. When she finished her coffee, I thanked her for coming and showed her to the door. The candidate scheduled for eleven a.m. didn't show up at all.

Eugene was getting as frustrated as I was. He offered to take me out to dinner when he got home Tuesday evening, but I declined. "The last couple of days have been so lousy and disappointing, I don't have much of an appetite," I told him. "I had no idea finding help for a few weeks would be this difficult," I complained. "Some of the women who come to the salon rave about their help. If I had more time, I could check with one of them and see if they could recommend somebody."

"Well, you still have a couple of days before you go in for surgery. In the meantime I'll check with some of my clients too." Eugene snorted and gave me a thoughtful look. "I wish . . ." He stopped and leaned back on our living-room couch with a mysterious expression on his face. I slumped at the other end.

"You wish what?" I asked.

"I wish we could find a woman like the one who worked for my family. Ethel Perkins was the best. She cooked, cleaned the house, and nursed Daddy back to health after his gallbladder surgery." Eugene chuckled. "Oh, that Ethel, that Ethel. She was such a world-beater! She'd put Mary Poppins to shame."

I gave him a bewildered look. "It's been decades since I saw that old movie, but wasn't Mary Poppins just a nanny?"

"Oh, Ethel filled that role too. She started taking care of Lawrence and me when we were still in elementary school."

"Hmm. Did you keep in touch with her?"

"No, I didn't, I'm sorry to say. After Lawrence and I left home, my folks retired. They no longer needed full-time domestic help. When they offered to let Ethel stay on a part-time basis, she turned them down. She had too many financial obligations, so a big cut in her pay didn't appeal to her. If I hadn't lost track of Ethel, I'd hire her in a heartbeat. The only thing is, she's got to be in her late sixties or early seventies by now and probably retired. She said that someday she'd love to move back to her hometown, Bugtussle, Kentucky. After all these years I doubt if she's even still in the L.A. area. She may have even changed her name." Eugene let out a loud breath and waved his hand. "What the heck! It's worth a shot. I'll see what I can find out."

He leaped from the couch and trotted out of the room. He returned fifteen minutes later with his laptop and a lined notepad. "I checked the telephone book and Google. There are several women named Ethel Perkins in the L.A. area. One is in her late nineties, one is eighty-six, and another one is only forty-four. We can eliminate those three off the bat. I made a list of the others."

After six calls and striking out, Eugene gave me a weary look and set his cell phone on the coffee table.

"Don't give up yet," I wailed, reaching for his cell phone and the list. I dialed the next-to-the-last number and a young boy answered. "Is this the residence of Ethel Perkins?" I asked.

"Yeah. She's not home yet," the boy replied.

"Was she ever employed as a housekeeper?"

"Yeah. She's still a housekeeper. Why are you asking me all these questions, lady?"

I gave Eugene a thumbs-up. His eyes got big and a wide smile formed on his face. "I think she's someone my husband used to know. He'd like to get in touch with her. Do you know if she worked for the Johnson family during the 1980s?"

"Huh?"

"I'm sorry. You probably wouldn't know that. Are there any adults in the house available to come to the phone?"

"Uh-uh."

"Do you expect Ethel home soon?"

"She's still at work, and . . . wait a minute, ma'am. She just walked in the door."

I heard some mumbling in the background and then a woman with a soft voice answered. "Can I help you?" she asked.

"Are you the Ethel Perkins who worked for the Johnson family some time ago in the Baldwin Hills area of L.A.?"

"Yes, I am. Why?"

"Hold on, please. There is someone here who is very anxious to talk to you," I said. My heart skipped a beat as I handed the telephone to Eugene. He pressed the speaker button.

"Ethel? Ethel Perkins, is it really you?"

There were a few moments of silence before she replied, "That's my name. Who are you people?"

"This is Eugene Johnson. Do you remember me?"

Ethel let out a yelp. "W-what? For goodness' sake! Boy, you and your rusty-butt brother gave me such a run for my money, I could *never* forget you with your hardheaded self!" She laughed. "How are your mama and daddy?"

"They passed several years ago," Eugene said in a somber tone.

"Oh, I'm sorry to hear that. I used to think about them and you and your brother all the time. What you been up to?"

Eugene brought Ethel up to date on his and his brother's activities and then he took a deep breath and told her the reason we'd called. He told her in great detail what she'd be required to do.

"Honey, I would love to nurse your wife back to health. But y'all called me at a bad time. Every Saturday, and some evenings during the week, I work the cash register at the convenience store at the end of the street I live on. On top of that, for the past eight years, I been cooking and cleaning for a lady named Mrs. Goldstein in Bel Air, Monday through Friday. She is in the process of going to live with her son in Maine. Me and her done packed up most of her stuff so she can be on her way by next Thursday. After next week I will be available for weekdays. But the thing is, I couldn't work for you and your wife temporarily. I need another full-time job. I been going on interviews for the past three weeks."

"You could work for us until you find another full-time job," Eugene said quickly.

"I don't think that's a good idea. I don't want to

start working for y'all and then get hired by somebody else and have to leave."

"Well, we would need for you to commit for the
full eight weeks. Okay, how about a compromise? If
you can commit to eight weeks, after that, you can
work for us as long as it takes for you to find another
full-time job," Eugene said.

"Oh yeah? The last time it took me seven months
to find a full-time job . . ."

"We don't care how long it takes," I blurted out.

"I declare. That sounds reasonable to me. I got a
couple of interviews lined up for next week, I can
cancel them."

"That would be wonderful. The only other thing
is, I'll be having my surgery this Friday. We would
need you to start on Monday. Would you be able to
do that?"

"I guess I could. Since I'm about to be laid off next
week, I'm sure Mrs. Goldstein won't mind if I don't
come back after this Friday."

"Good!" Eugene yelled, bumping my knee with
his. "But first you need to come over and meet with
Rosemary for an interview."

" 'An interview'?" Ethel hollered. "You called and
offered me a job point-blank, and now you telling me
I got to come over and *interview* first?"

"Oh no! The interview is just a formality. The job
is yours if you want it," I tossed in. "It's just that I

would like to meet you before you start. I was hoping you could come tomorrow morning around ten, or any other time during the day. If you can't make it tomorrow, you can come on Thursday, at any time."

"I'd rather come tomorrow. The lady that's fixing to lay me off has been good about letting me take off and interview for other jobs. Give me your address and I'll be there tomorrow whatever time you say—with bells on."

I told her what time to come, and I gave her our address.

"That went well," Eugene commented when we hung up.

"I'll say. She sounds very eager. I hope she's still as eager when I meet her."

"Ro, take my word for it. This woman will not be a disappointment."

When Eugene left the room, I called up Min-jee and told her everything Eugene had told me about his former "nanny."

"This Ethel sounds like a superwoman. I hope she lives up to your expectations," Min-jee said, sounding skeptical.

"I'm sure she will," I insisted.

"Be realistic now. The woman is up in age—"

I cut Min-jee off. "I was a little concerned about that, but then I talked to her. She should be okay for a couple of months."

Right after I ended the conversation with Min-jee, I called up Genelle. She said almost the same things Min-jee had said.

"I hope nobody else reminds me that the woman is elderly," I snapped, beginning to feel irritated. "I've hired her, and I am not going to renege. Besides, she's going to leave her other job a few days early to accommodate me."

"All right, now. Give me a call after you meet her. I'd like to know what you think about her then," Genelle said.

CHAPTER 9

I woke up before dawn on Wednesday morning. Despite how much Eugene had praised Ethel, I was still apprehensive. He hadn't communicated with her since he was in his teens. She could have changed a lot since then. Still, I had spoken to her and she sounded full of energy. And if she was still working two jobs, she had to be in good health. By the time I got out of bed, I was really looking forward to meeting her.

When she arrived at ten on the dot, I was surprised by the way she looked. She was not the stout woman I'd pictured in my mind. She was barely over five feet tall and couldn't have weighed more than 110 pounds. Her thick, gray hair was neatly styled in a French twist with bangs. The plaid duster she wore was so crisp and wrinkle-free, it looked brand-new. The only makeup she had on was maroon-colored lipstick. It was obvious that she had once been a very attractive woman, but lines and age spots had taken a toll on her honey-colored face.

"I hope you didn't have trouble finding the place," I said as I beckoned her into the living room.

"I didn't have no trouble at all," she said with a grin. "The bus driver gave me real good directions."

"Would you like a cup of coffee before we get started? I just made some and was about to have a cup myself."

"That would be nice. I take mine black."

"So do I. We'll talk in the kitchen."

I led her to the kitchen table and motioned her to a chair.

"You sure keep a nice, neat house, Mrs. Johnson." She gazed at the linoleum floor I had waxed two days ago. "And it smells so good up in here."

"Thank you. May I call you Ethel?"

"Please do."

"And please call me Rosemary."

"Yes, ma'am." This was the first time a woman old enough to be my mother addressed me in such a formal way. I was flattered.

"I am glad you were able to come at such short notice, and that you don't mind being interviewed. Like I told you when we spoke last night, this is just a formality. Eugene has told me so many wonderful things about you. And he's never wrong." I laughed and then I whispered, "Don't tell him I said that. He'd never let me forget it. His ego is big enough."

She chuckled. "That boy. He was a handful, him and his brother. But I am tickled to death to hear that he turned out so well. I declare, I never would have thought that he'd be a lawyer working with celebrities. Just goes to show that life is full of surprises. Um . . . I am surprised that you and him ain't got no kids. When he was a little boy, he used to tell me all the time how he was going to take his boys fishing, and to ball games, and to whatnot, when he had some. And how he was going to be very particular about the men his daughters got involved with."

"We tried for years to have children," I said in a dry tone as I filled two cups with coffee and set them on the table. "Things just didn't work out the way we thought they would." I sat down directly across from Ethel.

She lifted her cup and took a long pull before responding. "Well, you and Eugene still young enough. One of the ladies I used to work for some years ago didn't have her first child until she was forty-eight. Janet Jackson was fifty when she had her little boy. Don't give up."

I shook my head. "Unfortunately, I don't have a choice. The surgery I'm having will make it impossible for me to get pregnant. I'm having a hysterectomy."

"My Lord." Ethel gave me a sympathetic look, took a sip of her coffee and shook her head. "I had to have one right after I had my only child, a daughter. So I know how it feels."

"Yes. But at least you had one child. Does your daughter live in California?"

Ethel blinked hard and shook her head again. "She passed."

I gasped softly. "I am so sorry to hear that. Was she ill?"

"Something like that. She got pregnant when she was sixteen and had a baby girl herself. But she dropped out of school and got involved with the wrong crowd. Me and Harry, my late husband, we done all we could to get her back on the straight and narrow, but it didn't work. One night she went out and never came home. We filed a missing person's report, and a week later, they found her dead in a crack house in Watts."

"Oh, my," I mouthed. "Was it a drug overdose?"

"Somebody shot her. But if that hadn't killed her, them drugs would have done it eventually. She was so strung out, she didn't know which way was up."

"Was anybody ever arrested?"

"Uh-uh. All the folks she used to get high with claimed they didn't know nothing."

Ethel went on to tell me how she had to quit her job cleaning a cheap motel and stay home to take care of her granddaughter.

"That must have been hard on you and your husband."

"It was. But cleaning rooms in a seedy motel wasn't no picnic neither. I didn't make much money, and a lot of the people who checked into the rooms made it even worse. It was a haven for criminals and street-walkers. But every now and then, some halfway decent people checked in. A few even left me really big tips. Some of them was a caution to the wind though. One day a well-dressed man driving a great big Cadillac checked in for five days with his teenage daughter. He was on his way to Montana, he claimed. He was real friendly and polite. I liked him so much, I'd bring him extra bottles of water and shampoo. The last day he was there, I heard him tell his daughter, 'If you don't finish school, you're going to end up like her.' He was talking about me."

"He said that in front of you?"

"No, I was in the hallway getting him some more bottles of water and he didn't realize I was close enough to hear. That comment bothered me for days, so I was glad when I had to quit. What a lot of folks don't realize is that some of us don't have many choices. We have to take whatever jobs we can get."

"That's for sure." I heaved out a loud sigh. "Let's move on to something more uplifting. We're clear on the days and hours you need to be here, right?"

"Uh-huh. Monday through Friday, from nine a.m. to six p.m. Them is good days and hours. Almost the same ones I been working for years. Oh!" Ethel's face suddenly lit up like a lightbulb. "I brought my references." She pulled out a folded sheet of paper from her bamboo purse. "I know Mrs. Goldstein will say something good about me. She's a real religious Jewish lady, always looking to brighten somebody's day. She cried on the phone last night when I told her I couldn't help her finish her packing next week because I got a new job. But she wished me the best. I don't know about Smitty at the store where I work. He's so persnickety, he'd find fault with Jesus."

I laughed. "Don't worry about Smitty or Mrs. Goldstein. I won't be calling them. Eugene's 'reference' is enough for me."

We spent the next hour chatting about a variety of things. Then we drank another cup of coffee before Ethel glanced at her watch, sucked in some air, and gave me a pensive look. "I really enjoy sitting here, talking to you. But if you don't mind, can we finish up in a few minutes? Mrs. Goldstein gave me the whole day off and I'd like to get home and spend some time with my children. It would be nice to have dinner already cooked when they get home from school this afternoon."

"Children? I thought you only had the one granddaughter."

"I did for twenty-seven years. She also fell along the wayside and got involved with a rough crowd. Four years ago, she got stabbed to death in them streets. The day after her murder, they arrested the man who took her life. Now he's going to spend the rest of his behind bars."

At this point, Ethel stared off into space and her voice dropped to a whisper. "He was the son of my best friend. He found Jesus in San Quentin, and I eventually forgave him. Harboring hate is a heavy burden, and the longer you carry it, the heavier it gets. That's why I had to forgive him. It was the only way I could ease my pain. My granddaughter left behind three kids. Cynthia is fifteen now, Anthony is twelve, and Eddie just turned eleven last month. Their daddy had took off when Eddie was still in diapers. We ain't heard from him since. Me and Harry moved them in with us. When Harry died, bless his sweet soul, things got really tough. Even though I got a little bit of money from Social Security for the kids every month, working two jobs was the only way I could afford to move us out of that rough neighborhood in South Central to a safer one, before them kids got old enough for trouble to find them. We been living in a nice, quiet place in Inglewood for the past three years. I don't care what I have to do, I'm going to make sure them babies is safe."

"Those children are so lucky to have someone like you." I was getting emotional, so I was anxious for the interview to end now.

"No, the lucky one is me. Them kids done enriched my life in so many ways. I don't know what I'd do without them." Ethel paused and gave me a thoughtful look. "It ain't fair that a woman like you, who really wants kids and can give them such a good life, can't have none."

"Life is not fair. I have so many other blessings though. God's been so good to me."

"Well, if you keep the faith and let God do His job, you are going to have even more blessings," Ethel assured me with a nod. "What folks don't understand is that He may not give them what they want when they're ready for it. But He will give it to them when *He's* ready."

CHAPTER 10

Right after Ethel left, I called Eugene's office. He was in a meeting, so I left him a message and then I called the salon. Genelle answered. "How did the interview go?"

"It went quite well," I told her. "Ethel Perkins is perfect for me. I was thoroughly impressed by her."

"Oh yeah? What was it about her that impressed you so much?"

"Everything. She's very personable, warm, and eager to work. Not to mention the fact that Eugene had such a memorable experience with her when she worked for his family. Besides, she has a lot of experience. I can't wait to get to know her better." I was talking so fast, I had to stop and catch my breath. "Now tell me, is there anything going on there that I need to be aware of?"

"Well, yeah. Roxanne made an announcement this morning." Roxanne Pettigrew was one of the other four manicurists who worked for me.

"Uh-oh." I held my breath.

"Don't panic. It was good news. As you know, she and her boyfriend have been dating for more than fifteen years. He finally proposed last night, and she accepted. They are going to get married in Vegas next year on Valentine's Day."

"Whew! I thought you were going to tell me she's quitting. I'll give her a call later today and congratulate her. Anything else?"

"Just business as usual. Mrs. MacNeal showed up right after we opened, without an appointment *again*. She chipped two nails last night. As frantic as she was, you would have thought she'd broken her leg. When we refused to bump another client to accommodate her, she threatened to give us a bad review on Yelp. I offered to give up my lunch hour today so I could repair her nails, and that calmed her down. When I told her how chic she looked in her new mink stole, she got giddy and offered to let me spend a couple of free nights at her luxurious bed-and-breakfast whenever I want."

We frequently received lavish perks from our wealthy clients. Last month a talk show hostess treated me to a spa day at one of the most expensive establishments in town because I'd come to her house to do her nails.

"That Mrs. MacNeal. I hope her next appointment is with me." I laughed. "I wish the world could see what some of the *real* housewives of Beverly Hills are like and not go by what they see on those housewife reality shows on TV."

"Tell me about it. Anyway, I'm glad to hear that Ethel is the gem Eugene made her out to be."

"That sweet little woman has had her share of misery. Her husband's deceased. She lost her only child and only granddaughter to the streets when she lived in South Central. She's been working two jobs for years so she can afford to raise her granddaughter's three young children in a safer neighborhood. I felt sorry for her, but she didn't need any pity from me. I got the impression that she's a proud, resilient woman who can take care of her business on her own. And she has a very positive attitude. Being around such an upbeat person like her is just what I need."

Genelle sucked on her teeth and then snorted. "Oh yeah? Are you insinuating that Min-jee and I are not upbeat enough for you?"

"Don't put words in my mouth. You know what I mean."

"Yeah, I do. I'm just messing with you," she teased.

"Since I'm going to be out of commission for a while after this week, why don't you and Min-jee and I get together for a girls' night out before my surgery?"

"I'd like to, but Patrick and I and the kids are having dinner with his parents tomorrow. And Min-jee said something about having to attend her son's basketball game tonight. Listen, as soon as you get back on your feet, we'll do something real nice. I promise."

After I got off the phone, I called Eugene's office again. This time he was available. "How did it go with Ethel?" he asked.

"I love her already and can't wait to get to know her better. I can't put my finger on it, but as we were talking, there was something about her that made me feel special."

"Baby, you are special," Eugene assured me. "Would you like to go out to dinner this evening?"

"No. I had wanted to go out with Min-jee and Genelle. They have other plans. It's just as well. I need to conserve my strength for my surgery. But I don't feel like cooking . . ."

"All right. I can take a hint. I'll pick up some take-out on my way home."

"Thanks, honey. You know what else? Ethel reminds me of my mother."

"I can believe that. She reminds me of mine too."

"I have a feeling you won't lose track of her this time."

"Ro, I have the same feeling."

Eugene and I went to bed early Thursday night, but I didn't sleep much. Friday morning when I got up at seven, I was so tired I fell asleep in the car on the way to the medical center.

My surgery went off without a hitch. By Sunday afternoon I was doing so well, Dr. Miller authorized my release. When Eugene picked me up at three p.m., I was a little groggy, sore, and wobbly when they transferred me from a wheelchair to his SUV. But I was still in good spirits.

"I'm so glad it's over," I said in a voice so raspy that I sounded like a woman twice my age. "I can't wait to go back to work."

"Work is the last thing you need to be thinking about right now," he scolded as he eased out of the hospital parking lot. "You're going to follow Dr. Miller's orders to the letter."

Eugene carried me into the house and gently placed me on the living-room couch. Min-jee and Genelle had keys to our house, so they had already let themselves in.

"You know I'm just a phone call or a text message away. You can get in touch with me anytime, day or night, and I'll be here in a flash," Genelle said, hovering over me.

"The same goes for me," Min-jee added. She stood next to Genelle with her hands on her hips.

"Thank you, ladies," Eugene said. He stood at the foot of the couch with a weary look on his face. There were dark circles around his eyes, and I knew he hadn't slept much in the last couple of days. He'd slept on a cot in my hospital room Friday and Saturday night. "Ethel's going to start tomorrow. But if we need extra help, I won't hesitate to call."

While Genelle and Min-jee were chatting with Eugene, I fell into a deep sleep. When I woke up, it was dark outside, and I was still on the couch. Eugene was slumped in a chair facing me. He had changed from the polo shirt and black pants he'd worn earlier and was now in his pajamas.

"I must look a fright," I complained, running my fingers through my matted hair and looking around the room as I sat up. "Where are Min-jee and Genelle?"

"They left about an hour ago."

"Why did you let me sleep so long?"

"Rosemary, you need to get as much sleep and rest as you can."

"Yeah. You're right, I guess."

"Min-jee made some soup before she left," Eugene said, sitting with his legs crossed and an uneasy expression on his face.

"That was nice of her. But I don't feel like eating anything at the moment. Save it for later. Did I get any calls?" I looked at the landline on the end table, then at my cell phone on the coffee table.

"A few church members and Reverend Updike checked to see how you were getting along. He wanted to know when he'd see us in church again."

"We were there two Sundays ago. And every Sunday before then for the past three months."

"I told him we probably wouldn't be back until you're fully recovered. He said that if we need some spiritual guidance in the meantime, give him a call. He'd be glad to come to the house with his prayer team."

"That's good to know. Did anybody else call?"

"A few neighbors and all four of those other manicurists who work for you. By the way, you have get-well cards from all the same people. And Ethel called a few minutes ago."

I was glad to hear that so many people had called to check on me and sent cards. But when I heard Ethel's name, I let out a sharp gasp. "What did she say?" I hoped she hadn't called to tell us she wouldn't be able to come tomorrow after all.

Eugene must have read my mind because he held up his hand and chuckled before I could say anything else. "Don't look so panicked. She just called to check up on you and to say that she's looking forward to getting started tomorrow morning."

"Thank God. I'm glad to hear that," I managed, wiping sweat off my forehead.

"Baby, are you comfortable? Do you want me to get a couple of pillows for you?"

"No, that's okay. Lying on the couch is nice, but I'd like to sleep upstairs tonight."

Eugene insisted on sleeping in one of the other bedrooms for a while so I could have the whole king-size bed in our room to myself. He was a restless sleeper.

Some nights he tossed, turned, and flailed his arms and legs so much that I woke up with bruises. That never bothered me. But under the current circumstances, I didn't think sharing the same bed with such a combative sleeper was a smart thing for me to do.

An hour later, I felt like eating. I ate a bowl of the delicious shrimp soup Min-jee had prepared and some saltine crackers. Then I consumed about a quart of water to wash down the large pain capsules I had to take to ease some of my discomfort.

They'd given me a sponge bath before I left the hospital. However, I had sweated so much, I didn't feel clean anymore. I was too wobbly to stand under a shower and too sore to sit in the bathtub, so Eugene gave me another sponge bath before he put me to bed.

I slept like a baby that night, and when I woke up Monday morning a few minutes before nine o'clock, Ethel Perkins was standing next to Eugene with a wall-to-wall smile on her face. I smiled too, looking from her to Eugene.

"I feel so much better," I wheezed. I almost felt like my old self until I attempted to sit up. A sharp pain shot from the top of my stomach all the way down to my hips.

Eugene gasped. But before he could speak, Ethel placed her hands on my shoulders and gently pushed me back down. "Lie still, sugar."

"But I feel okay. I don't want to just lie here like a deadweight," I said with a pout.

"You don't have to do anything as long as I'm here." She whirled around and gazed at Eugene. "Son, why don't you go on to your office. We'll be just fine."

Eugene checked his watch. I didn't give him a chance to protest. "Honey, please leave so Ethel and I can start getting acquainted."

"All right, then," he mumbled after giving me a mournful look.

The minute he left, Ethel dragged the stool from my vanity table to the side of the bed and sat down. "I'll get you sponged off a bit and then I'll fix you some breakfast. What would you like?"

"I'm sorry, Ethel. I told you all you'd have to prepare was my lunch and an afternoon snack now and then. After today Eugene will fix breakfast for me before he leaves. I guess it skipped his mind this morning because you're here."

"Oh, I don't mind. Whenever he don't have time to cook, I'll be glad to do it. Shoot, you can let him know right off that I'll do the breakfast each morning."

"Okay. This morning I'd like some grits and scrambled eggs cooked well done. I like diced jalapeno peppers with my eggs."

"What a coincidence. That's how I like my eggs too," Ethel squealed.

I was somewhat disoriented and my ability to gauge time was off. That was why I couldn't determine how long it had taken Ethel to return to my room with a tray. It contained a bowl of chicken salad, two slices of wheat toast, a banana cut in half, and a glass of warm milk. "That's a hearty-looking breakfast. I was expecting grits and eggs," I said, chuckling.

"This ain't breakfast, it's lunch," Ethel responded, setting the tray in front of me. "When I brought up the grits and eggs with jalapeno peppers scrambled up in them, you was out like a light. That was several hours ago."

I glanced at the clock on my nightstand, surprised to see that it was five minutes past one p.m. "I've been asleep all this time?" I croaked.

"Sure enough," Ethel said, nodding firmly. "Them ladies that work for you been calling and calling all day. The lady professor who lives next door dropped by. I told her to come back tomorrow. By then, you should have most of your bearings back."

"What about Eugene? Has he called since he left for work?"

"Pffftt!" Ethel gave me a dismissive wave. "Honey, that man done called every half hour since he left this house. I told him for the umpteenth time he ain't got to worry about nothing as long as I'm here. And you ain't neither."

By the end of the second day with Ethel, I was so attached to her, I didn't want her to leave.

Our telephone rang continually with calls from our

church family, neighbors, relatives, and other well-wishers. Receiving so much love and support made me feel better. But nothing could ease the pain of knowing I'd never have a child now. It wasn't easy, but each time the thought entered my mind, I pushed it to the back. But it always managed to ease back to the front.

CHAPTER 11

It had been five days since my surgery. I felt strong enough to get out of bed and teeter from my bed to the bathroom on my own and not use the wheelchair we had rented. But a few times I had to hold on to Ethel's or Eugene's arm.

My stomach was not as swollen as it had been the days before and I didn't feel nearly as weak, sore, and clumsy. I wobbled up out of bed Wednesday morning, anxious to go downstairs for the first time since Sunday. I'd just finished the oatmeal and toast Eugene had prepared.

Ethel hadn't arrived yet. I could hear Eugene downstairs talking to someone on the telephone. I felt a little light-headed and had to take baby steps, so it took me a while to make it to the living room. As soon as Eugene spotted me, he ended his call and dashed across the room.

"Rosemary, you shouldn't be moving about too much on your own yet," he scolded, grabbing my arm and steering me to the couch.

"I'm fine," I insisted, easing down. "If I lie in that bed too much longer, I'm going to develop bedsores."

"That's better than you falling and injuring yourself!" he blasted as he eased down next to me and smoothed my limp hair back with his hand.

"Oh, hush!" I shot back. I rolled my eyes and changed the subject. "Who were you talking to on the phone?"

"Randy McFarland. He called to tell me that he won't be able to go fishing this Saturday like we'd planned. His in-laws suddenly decided to fly down from Sacramento for Thanksgiving. They'll arrive this Friday and his wife wants him to stay close to home as long as they're in town."

"I'm sorry you won't be able to go. I know how much you were looking forward to it."

"It's just as well. If he hadn't canceled, I probably would have. I wasn't sure how well you'd be doing. Randy said that if I change my mind, I can use his boat and go by myself. You're welcome to tag along, if you feel up to it."

"Ha! I don't care how good I feel this weekend, I am not going out on a fishing boat to sit around and watch you fiddle with bait and drink beer."

"I didn't think so," Eugene said, chuckling.

"But you should still go. Ask one of your other friends to join you. You'll only be gone for a few hours, and Min-jee and Genelle are just a phone call away in case I need something before you return."

"I just don't like going fishing by myself, and everybody else I know has plans for Saturday. I'll just hold off until I find somebody who'd like to go with me."

Before we could continue the conversation, Ethel knocked on the front door. Eugene sprang up off the couch and darted to the door to let her in.

"Rosemary, why are you out of bed?" she hollered as she rushed over to me, with Eugene trailing close behind.

"Because she's hardheaded," he accused.

"I couldn't stay in that bed another minute," I whined. "Ethel, you can bring my pillows and a blanket down here, because this is where I'm going to spend the next few days."

Turned out, the couch was not nearly as comfortable as my bed. Less than an hour after Eugene left, I had Ethel help me back to my bedroom.

A few hours later, after I'd eaten the tomato soup and ham sandwich Ethel had served me in bed for lunch, I called for her to come remove the tray. She didn't answer. I waited a few minutes and called her name again, much louder. She still didn't answer.

I set the tray on my nightstand and eased out of bed. Despite the fact that I had felt better earlier, I immediately felt drowsy and had to flop back down on the side of the bed. After a few moments I attempted to stand again. I didn't feel drowsy at all this time, so I plucked my bathrobe from the foot of the bed and crept back downstairs.

The TV was on in the living room, so I headed in that direction. I did a double take when I got there. Ethel was slumped over on the couch, sleeping like a baby, with the handle of the vacuum cleaner still in her hand.

"Ethel!" I yelled as I rushed toward her.

Her eyes flew open before I even reached the couch. "Huh? Oh! I'm sorry, Rosemary. I just dozed off for a few minutes," she explained.

"Are you all right?" I asked, rubbing her shoulder.

"Honey, I'm fine. I was just a little tired."

"Do you want to go back home? I'll call Uber or Lyft."

Ethel's mouth dropped open and her eyes got big. "Goodness no! I can't leave you in this house by yourself!"

"Don't worry about me. I'm doing just fine," I insisted. "I'll stay off my feet until Eugene gets home." My heart was beating so hard, it felt like it was trying to burst out of my chest.

"You doing 'just fine' because I'm here to help you get around," she pointed out, chuckling. "Now I ain't never slacked up on no job, I ain't about to start now." She stood up and folded her arms. "Now let's get you back upstairs to that bed."

I returned to my room and got back in bed. Ethel sat in the wing chair I kept by the side of the bed. For the next couple of hours, we chatted about events in the news, TV shows we did and didn't like, and she shared some interesting stories about some of her relatives back in Bugtussle, Kentucky. Most of them were humorous, so I encouraged her to continue.

"The year before I moved to California, my uncle Peter lost one of his arms in a car wreck. But he was so handsome, he could still get girlfriends—even though he was already married. His wife, Clara, was way taller than him and outweighed him by at least a hundred pounds," she shared. "When she caught him with another woman one day, she grabbed him by his arm, lifted him up off the ground, and swung him around until he screamed bloody murder. He was so dizzy by the time she turned him loose, it took two of my other uncles to hold him up."

"My God!" I exclaimed. "That must have been horrible for him."

"It was, but it didn't stop him from fooling around. He wasn't so lucky when she caught him the next time. After she gave him a good whupping, she left him for a blind man. But the one that really takes the cake is my cousin Melinda. She's been married so many times, she can't keep track of her exes. When she got married again last year, she didn't know that the man she was marrying was one she'd been married to before! He had been her first husband. She and him so senile now, they didn't realize that until our cousin Annie Ruth pointed it out to them."

"How many times has your cousin been married?" Ethel gave me a thoughtful look and actually counted, using her fingers. "Teddy will make it ten. But since they'd already been married once, I'm counting him twice." We laughed.

"Eugene is the only man for me," I said proudly. "If something happens to him, I probably would never remarry."

"I felt the same way when my husband died. Good men like my Harry was, is as scarce as hen's teeth. I had no desire to try and find a replacement. I'm so grateful I got them kids to keep me company in my old age."

No matter how hard I tried to avoid the subject of my not having children, it always seemed to come up. It didn't matter if it was directly, or indirectly, I didn't want to talk about it. I quickly changed the subject. "Would you mind fixing me a cup of coffee? It helps me from feeling drowsy."

"In that case I better have a cup myself," she answered, rising from her chair with a groan. "Um, Rosemary, please don't tell Eugene you caught me sleeping on the job."

"What?"

"I really need this job. I don't want you and Eugene to think y'all made a mistake by hiring me when you could have got somebody younger and more able."

"Ethel, you don't have to worry about getting fired. We asked you to stay until my doctor tells me I'm well enough to fend for myself and can go back to work. You're doing everything we hired you for. That's all that matters." I paused. "But I don't want you to get sick trying to help me get well."

"Oh, I ain't sick. Like I said, I was just tired. I didn't get much sleep last night. Every night before I go to bed, I check on the kids to make sure they are all tucked in and done said their prayers. Well, the boys was fine. But while I was checking on them, Cynthia snuck out of the house. She started doing that last year. Anyway, I sat up last night until she came home, which was after midnight. When I asked her where she'd been, all she told me was that she had been 'out with friends' and to mind my own business."

This was the first time Ethel mentioned having problems with any of her great-grandchildren.

"I'm sorry to hear that."

There was a glazed look in her eyes as she continued speaking. "I love that child to death, but I don't know how much longer I can tolerate her obnoxious behavior. I never had that kind of trouble with her mama, so I can't understand how she turned out this way."

"I thought you said your granddaughter got involved with a bad crowd."

"She did, but she was over eighteen by then. She never tried to hide it, so I knew from the get-go what I was dealing with. I never know what to expect from Cynthia, and she ain't but fifteen. One minute she seems fine and more than willing to help me take care of the house and the boys. Then the next thing I know, she's gone for days at a time. When she comes home, she tells me over and over she don't like being told what to do." Ethel paused and let out a loud breath. "Rosemary, I'm doing everything I can to keep the girl out of trouble."

"Has she been in any serious trouble, other than running away?"

"Not yet."

"Maybe losing her mother to violence has something to do with her behavior."

"You're probably right. She never wants to talk about her mama and how she died. When it comes up, she goes around for days on end, mad at the world." Ethel shook her head and waved her hands in the air. "Let me shut my mouth . . ."

"You don't have to stop talking. I don't mind listening at all. It doesn't help to keep things bottled up inside. Do you want to talk about Cynthia some more?"

Ethel shook her head. "No, I don't. And I wish I hadn't brought her up. I don't like to dump my problems on nobody."

"If you do want to talk more about her, the boys, or anything else, don't hesitate. And if there is anything I can do, I'd be more than happy to help."

"Thanks for letting me know that, Rosemary. I got a feeling I may have to take you up on that someday."

CHAPTER 12

Eugene stayed home from work on Thursday so he could drive me to the medical center for my annual visit with Dr. Nash, my general practitioner, and my follow-up visit with Dr. Miller afterward. My first appointment wasn't until one p.m.

"I'll stay here until y'all get back," Ethel offered as we prepared to leave the house at noon.

"You don't have to do that. We may do some shopping and have dinner before we come home. You can take the rest of the day off and we'll see you in the morning," Eugene told her.

Ethel blinked and pressed her lips together. "But I ain't been here but three hours!" she wailed. "I can't afford to be taking off early. I need all the money I can get."

"We'll still pay you for the whole day," Eugene assured her, patting her shoulder.

She breathed a sigh of relief, but she continued to protest. "Honest to God, I don't mind staying here by myself. I'm sure I can find something to do to keep myself busy. Or I could watch a few TV shows. Mrs. Goldstein used to leave me in her house alone for six or seven hours while she went shopping or to long lunches with her friends."

"Ethel, if you want to just sit here alone, you're welcome to it. But I'm letting you know up front, you don't have to," Eugene said in a firmer tone. "Now I appreciate all you do for us, but you deserve unexpected breaks like everybody else."

"He's right, Ethel," I chimed in as I checked my makeup in the mirrored wall facing the couch. "If you don't want to go home, treat yourself to a movie or something. If anybody deserves to be pampered, it's you."

"All right, then. I just don't ever want y'all to think I'm taking advantage of this sweet position I'm in already."

Eugene and I looked at each other and then at Ethel. "We would never think that. Now go get your coat. We can drop you off anywhere you want," he said, already reaching for his jacket on the coatrack.

We dropped Ethel off at Sizzler on Manchester Boulevard. She'd chosen it because it was close enough for her to walk home after she ate lunch. "I ain't ate here since Harry died. He took me here for my birthday," she said as she piled out of Eugene's SUV. "Thank y'all. This was a good choice."

"Enjoy your lunch, Ethel. We'll see you tomorrow," Eugene said.

We didn't leave the parking lot until she entered the restaurant. "It sure doesn't take much to make her happy," I commented as we headed back into traffic. "I wonder if she's always been this humble."

"I don't know if 'humble' is the right word. She's a proud woman. When she worked for my parents, she refused to take handouts."

"Handouts?"

"Well, Mama used to try and pass on some of her old clothes and household items to Ethel instead of donating them to charity. But Ethel would fuss about it and claim she didn't need any of those things. Mama eventually stopped. A lot of our neighbors complained about their servants stealing from them, drinking up their booze, and even neglecting and mistreating their kids. They always got caught right away. We never had a problem with Ethel misbehaving. As lax as we were, she could have really taken us for a long ride. One time I dropped a hundred-dollar bill in my room and she put it in an envelope and gave it to my mother. She is one of the most genuinely good people I ever met. I wish we had more friends like her."

I squinted at Eugene. "So you think of our servant as a friend?"

He whirled around to face me with his mouth hanging open. "Don't you?"

I dropped my head for a moment. Then I looked up at him with a sheepish grin. "Of course, I do," I admitted, gently punching the side of his arm. "Let's get on to the medical center."

"Rosemary, I am pleased to see that you are doing so well," Dr. Nash exclaimed after he'd examined me. He cleared his throat and raked his fingers through his thin white hair. "Your blood pressure is still a little higher than it should be, but it's lower than it was the last time you were here, so continue taking the pills I have you on now. Unfortunately, I don't like the level of your cholesterol. I'm going to give you a stronger prescription for that today."

"But I feel fine," I protested.

"That doesn't mean a thing. There are a lot of people in the cemeteries who felt 'fine.'"

Like Dr. Miller, Dr. Nash had been taking care of me for almost twenty years, so I was very comfortable with him. Not only was he charming and easy to talk to, he had a dry sense of humor. I could say anything within reason, and he wouldn't feel offended.

"That's pretty ominous." I laughed. He didn't.

"So is high blood pressure and high cholesterol," he said in a very serious tone. "This is not a casual matter, so don't make light of it. I'm going to keep a close watch on both conditions. Therefore, I'd like to see you again in two months. Make an appointment with my receptionist before you leave."

My visit to Dr. Miller was a little more positive. "Mrs. Johnson, you're doing better than I expected," he told me with a grin. "But I still advise you to take it fairly easy for at least another month. I don't think you'll need the woman who's been looking after you too much longer. If you don't belong to a gym, I suggest you buy yourself a membership. If you don't want to do that, start jogging in a couple of weeks, or purchase some exercise equipment and work out at home."

I blinked at Dr. Miller and sniffed. "Um . . . I'll do that. But I think, for a little while longer, I'll keep the lady who has been helping me. She could use the money."

That statement was true, but it really seemed like I wouldn't need Ethel's help the full six to eight weeks. However, I planned to keep her around that long, and even longer if I could.

I noticed sadness in Ethel's eyes immediately when she arrived Friday morning. And she was moving a lot slower than she usually did. A few minutes before ten a.m., I entered the kitchen, where she was wiping off the counter.

"You don't need to worry about that, remember?" I reminded. "Min-jee is coming over this evening."

"I don't mind. I don't feel right sitting around doing nothing," she insisted. "I was just about to come see if you wanted some coffee or something."

"No thanks. But I would like to talk to you about something."

Ethel drew a sharp breath. "You ain't pleased with my work?"

I shook my head and waved my hand. "That's not it. I want you to stay even after I go back to work."

"Say what?"

"If you're happy here and want to stay, I'd like for you to stay on permanently. I'm sure Eugene wants you to stay longer too."

"W-why, Mrs. Johnson—"

"Rosemary. We're on a first-name basis here, remember?"

"Yes, Mrs.—Rosemary. I would love to stay on with you and Eugene. You don't know how much easier working for y'all has made my life. The money sure is helping us out a lot, and I know the kids will be tickled to death when I tell them you want me to stay on. But I need to let you know that I got another mess brewing that could throw a monkey wrench in everything."

"I'm sorry to hear that. If you'd rather find another permanent job, I understand."

"That ain't it. And to tell you the truth, I doubt if I ever will find another permanent, full-time job. Maybe I can get on at another one of them cheap motels again. But when it comes to housekeeping jobs and whatnot, folks is real leery about hiring a woman my age these days. The only reason I was still with

Mrs. Goldstein was because I'd been with her so long, and she didn't like being in that big old mansion by herself. But there is something else I need to let you know."

"What is it?"

"I'm concerned about finding a new place to live."

I was under the impression that Ethel loved where she lived. What she'd just said threw me for a loop. "You want to move?"

"I don't want to move, but I might not have no choice. See, our building was sold a few weeks ago. The last time that happened in another place where we was living at, the new owner jacked up the rent so high, I couldn't afford to pay it. We had to move. If the church hadn't come through and helped me with the first and last months' rent for a new place, and a security deposit in the same amount as the rent, me and them kids would have been on the street."

"What about your family?"

"I love my family. They are some of the most up-standing, God-fearing people in the world. But life ain't been too good to them. They struggling just to get by these days. I can't expect no help from them. I just hope the new owner will give me enough time to find a new place I can afford. My building manager said it could be three or four months before he makes any changes."

"Is that why you're looking so sad today?"

"Uh-huh. Partly. Working two jobs, and now having to worry about moving, is about to drive me nuts."

"Tell you what," I chirped. "If you don't find a place by the time you have to move, you can always stay with us until you do."

Ethel gasped so hard, she choked on some air. She had to cough and clear her throat before she could continue. "Excuse me? *Me?* Stay here in this big, beautiful home?"

"Yes."

"B-but my kids—"

"They can come too."

Ethel gave me an incredulous look and dropped her head. She stared at the floor for a few seconds. "That's real sweet of you, Rosemary. But I pray to God it don't come to that. I'd have a real mess on my hands. Them kids would pout up a storm. They love where we live and the schools they go to. They would not want to leave their friends. On top of that, our church is close enough we can walk to it. And the friends I ain't outlived, or that ain't in nursing homes, still reside over there. If I don't find a place in the same neighborhood, the kids would be as disappointed as I would be. But I'll put that on the back burner for now and concentrate on something else that's eating at me."

"Oh? Is there something else you want to tell me?"

"Rosemary, I ain't no spring chicken. You knew that before y'all even called me up. I'm worried to death about what's going to happen to the kids when

I'm gone. It's on my mind all the time now. That's one of the reasons I don't sleep so good no more."

"Come on now. You're in great health. Why are you even talking about something like that?"

"Yeah, I'm in 'great health,' but I'm also in my last years. I'll be seventy years old in January."

"That's not so old."

"Maybe not to people your age. But as far as folks my age is concerned, if I was just sixty or sixty-five, that's still right old. I pray every night that the good Lord will let me stay around until the kids finish high school."

"And I'm sure He'll do just that."

"Don't try and second-guess God. He takes you when He's ready, not when you ready." Ethel sniffed, tilted her head to the side, and continued. "My niece Vernell said she'd take the boys. She's got six already, so she and her husband don't think two more would make too much of a difference. But Cynthia's been quite disrespectful to Vernell and her husband lately, and now they don't want to deal with her."

"What about some of your other relatives?"

"Like I said, they all struggling too much already. My cousin Jackson helped me a lot when my husband died. Him and his wife is fixing to move out of the hood because of all the violence and break-ins. Their names is on two waiting lists for one of them assisted-living facilities. They said they'll take the first one that calls them."

"Do you still have family in Kentucky? Maybe they could help out."

"Lordy, Lordy, Lordy! Most of them stay waaaaaay up in the backcountry and still live the same way folks in the South lived when I was a young girl. Sending kids that done lived in a sophisticated place like California all their lives to a place like Bugtussle would be like sending them to a different planet. Not only is my folks back there behind the times, almost every single one is so superstitious that they scared of anything modern. Even cable television and ATMs! The kids might be safer back there, but they'd never adjust to that lifestyle. If I had left that hick town sooner, I might have finished high school out here. Then I could have got a job in an office, or Walmart, or in a factory. I want my kids to have more opportunities than I had. California is the best state for that, in my book."

"I won't argue with that. Well, I hope you work things out so that they can stay in California."

"I done turned it over to the Lord. If they have to go live in foster homes, I'm sure He'll find good ones for them."

"Don't worry about that. Eugene and I took in a couple of foster children a few years ago. They loved living with us as much as we loved having them."

Ethel paused and gazed at me for a few moments. "Well, I hope if it comes to that, they end up with foster parents like y'all."

CHAPTER 13

Unless Eugene had to meet with a client after regular business hours, he usually got home about twenty or thirty minutes before Ethel left for the day. Of course, tonight was one of the later nights—when I couldn't wait to tell him what she had shared with me a few hours ago.

Right after she left to go catch her bus, he came home. Within seconds after he dropped his briefcase on the coffee table and flopped down on the couch, I sat down next to him.

"How was your day?" I asked.

"Same old grind," he replied in a tired tone. He moaned and leaned back while I gently massaged his tense shoulder. "Everybody wants everything, and they want it now. Remember that soap actress I took on two months ago?"

I hunched my shoulders. "I'm not sure. Except for the fabulous Joan Collins on the cable TV reruns we watch of that old nighttime soap *Dynasty*, they all sound alike to me. Why do you ask?"

"Humph. I should be lucky enough to work with a lady like Joan Collins. It's because she's got so much class that she's still working in her middle eighties. The one I'm referring to has already become a major thorn in my side. After all the back-and-forth hassling with the soap's producers, she wants to renegotiate her contract and ask for more money. She thinks because she's appeared in a few indie movies, she should get more."

"What's wrong with that?" I stopped massaging his shoulder and sat up straighter.

"Well, for one thing, this crybaby has only been on the soap for a year. Before that, she hadn't worked in over two years. I tried to explain to her that she's lucky to be working at all."

I gave Eugene a puzzled look. "Is it because of her age or color?" I read the trade magazines Eugene kept around the house, and I watched enough talk shows to know how cruel the entertainment industry could be, especially to older and minority women.

"Neither. She's a twenty-five-year-old blue-eyed blonde originally from Sweden."

"Then she must not be very attractive."

"She's gorgeous. Her problem is her attitude. She thinks the world should cater to her. That's what happens when parents spoil a child. And from what she's told me, her folks treated her like a princess."

"Treating a child like royalty usually does more harm than good. Discipline, love, proper guidance, and luck are what it takes to keep them grounded. But there could be a lot of other factors responsible for Miss Soap Opera's divalike behavior."

"Maybe so. The meeting I had with her and her agent this morning wore me down to a frazzle. And I'll be meeting with her again the day after Thanksgiving," Eugene said with a sluggish shrug. He perked up so fast, it made my head spin. "Something sure smells good." He sniffed and glanced toward the kitchen.

"I told Ethel you could cook when you got home, but she insisted on cooking that pot roast I defrosted."

"That was nice of her. She's really on the ball, huh?"

"That's for sure. She told me she likes to keep busy. She even insisted on rearranging my closet and steam cleaning the hallway carpet upstairs today. If she wants to cook breakfast and dinner for us too, from time to time, I'm not going to stop her."

"Good! I'm glad she hasn't changed much. She wore a lot of hats when I was growing up. Would you believe that she used to bathe and feed the rottweiler that Lawrence and I rescued from the street? We got out of doing a lot of chores because of Ethel, but Mama put her foot down the day she caught her mowing the lawn she'd been bugging me to do for a whole week!" Eugene laughed. "I'm sure that pot roast she cooked will taste better than if I had cooked it. I had a light lunch today, so I hope it's a big one."

"It'll be more than enough for the two of us, and we'll have a lot left over. Before we eat, I need to talk to you about something else first." I shifted in my seat and sucked in a deep breath.

Eugene gave me a cautious look. "Oh? What about?"

He listened with his face looking as stiff as stone as I told him everything Ethel had told me. When I stopped talking, there was an unbearably sad look on his face.

"I'm sorry to hear all that. But I wish you had talked to me first before you invited her to move in with us."

"You don't want to help her?" I wailed.

"I'd love to help her. But taking in an elderly woman and three young kids is a big responsibility, baby."

"We have four empty bedrooms."

"That's not what I'm talking about. Ethel might jump at the chance to move in, but what about those kids? You just said she told you they wouldn't want to leave their schools and friends. Not even temporarily."

"I know. But we'll work around that. They are still minors and have to do whatever Ethel tells them to do.

If she can't find a place she can afford before the new owner raises the rent, she could end up in a shelter."

"Oh, come on! It won't come to that. Ethel is too smart and resilient to let that happen. She's always been able to take care of her responsibilities."

"A lot of changes take place when a person reaches her age. If she gets sick or something, those kids could end up with her relatives. They are all struggling to take care of their own kids. Or they could end up in foster homes. If that happens, they'll probably be separated."

"I wouldn't want to see any of that happen. But Ethel still has plenty of years left, so I don't know why we're even discussing this. Besides, we have to give her credit for doing so much to keep them on the straight and narrow now. I'm sure she's raising them well. No matter where they end up, I am confident that they will continue to flourish."

"Then you're telling me you don't want them to move in with us?"

Eugene gave me an exasperated look. "Don't twist my words. I didn't say that. I'm trying to get you to keep this situation in the proper perspective. If they were to move in with us and something happened to Ethel, we wouldn't have any legal rights as to the fate of the children. They'd end up with relatives or in foster care anyway. That would add to their trauma." Eugene moaned and rubbed his forehead. "Look, I've been bombarded enough with drama for one day. Do you mind if we discuss this again later? Like in a day or so?"

"Sure."

"Good. I think we'll have a better perspective on it then. Now let's go dig into that pot roast."

CHAPTER 14

It rained heavily the following Tuesday. Around three p.m., after my sixth telephone call from Eugene, and half as many from Min-jee and Genelle, Ethel entered the living room. I was lying on the couch, enjoying a cup of tea. She was holding a bucket that contained water and a sponge. She insisted on wiping down the kitchen appliances every other day.

"Why don't you put that bucket down and sit down for a while? You've been up and about since you walked in the door," I said, waving her to the love seat across from me.

"Well, for a few minutes, I guess." She plonked down and set the bucket on the floor next to her feet.

"Ethel," I began. "You sound and look tired. More than you did last week. It's all right if you need to take a few days off. I can fend for myself."

"Good gracious no, Rosemary. I agreed to stay for eight weeks *every day,* and that's what I'm going to do. Unless you want me to leave after all . . ."

I sat up and set my cup on the coffee table. "We don't want you to leave. And I still think you should seriously consider moving in with us."

"I done thought about it and that sounds like too much for me to put on you and Eugene's plate. It wouldn't be so bad if it was just me. But coming with three kids, I'd feel so—"

I immediately cut Ethel off. "You don't have to feel so anything. You didn't ask to move in with us, I asked you. But if you don't want to, I'd be more than happy to help you find a place. It would give me something to do so I won't feel so useless sitting and lying around the house with you waiting on me hand and foot. And I would even take care of your moving expenses."

Ethel's eyes got big and her lips quivered. "Rosemary, I can't let you do all that neither!"

"I'd like to do that and more. I will leave the invitation to move in with us on the table." I ignored the fact that Eugene had told me to give this issue more thought. I knew that in the end he'd go along with whatever I wanted to do.

"There is another reason I don't think us moving in here would work out. The boys wouldn't be no trouble, but Cynthia would give y'all a run for your money. She wants to do whatever she wants, when she wants."

"Does her behavior have anything to do with boys?"

"No. She don't seem too interested in them yet. She's got a problem with her attitude and wearing clothes that sends out the wrong message. Low-cut tops, tight britches, and whatnot. I done lost count of how many times I had to go see her school counselor in the last few months about something she said or done, or something she wore to school. I don't buy her no hoochie-coochie clothes, but she always manages to borrow some from her friends."

"She's a teenager growing up in Los Angeles. Dressing inappropriately and having a bad attitude comes with the territory. We were all teenagers once."

"True. Lord knows I wasn't no angel when I was her age. I dropped out of school, got myself pregnant, and run off to California with a man who didn't have nothing to offer but hisself. But I never mouthed off to my mama the way Cynthia do to me sometimes. She likes school, but when she's there, she spends more time socializing than learning. Somehow she still manages to be on the honor roll. But that don't keep her from acting up. Trying to talk some sense into her don't do much good. She keeps telling me to let her live her life the way she wants to. I'm just scared to death that I'm going to lose her too."

"Please get that thought out of your head." I wanted to get up and go give Ethel a hug. I couldn't do that, because I didn't want her to know just how concerned I was about her, but I was showing more concern than I wanted to anyway.

"The last time I had to go see that school counselor, she advised me to take Cynthia to talk to a therapist. I took her to a woman associated with the Social Security folks because they send me benefits for the kids. Well, that quacky woman didn't do much good. Cynthia told me she spent most of her sessions fiddling around on her cell phone. Sound like to me, the therapist needed some therapy. Anyway, nothing changed. If anything, the situation got worse because Cynthia lost hope in therapy." Ethel moaned and rubbed her head. "I declare, I'm almost at the end of my rope with that girl."

"There are better therapists available. Eugene's parents took him to one when he was acting up, and look how he turned out."

"It must have been a good one if they was able to straighten him out. I remember how he used to skip school, miss his curfew, mouth off, and act a fool in front of his mama and daddy like he had lost his mind. I'd love to get Cynthia to a real good therapist. But they cost money. The government only pays for the ones they approve, like the one that didn't do Cynthia no good."

"I could find a good professional to talk to her. One of the ladies who comes to my salon counsels a lot of troubled celebrities. She's had a lot of success helping them turn their lives around. I am sure she'd be able to help Cynthia."

"Aw, Rosemary. That is so generous of you. God's got His eye on you, woman. Mark my word, He's going to bless you in ways you never imagined." Ethel paused and glanced out the window and then back at me with a hopeful look on her face. "But don't wear yourself out on my account. You doing too much already just by keeping a rickety old woman like me on the payroll. Let me hush. I keep saying I don't want to burden you with my problems, and that's just what I'm doing."

"You're not burdening me. You can share anything you want with me. By the way, you can take tomorrow and the rest of the week off."

"Oh? But Thanksgiving is day after tomorrow. And you don't want me to come on Friday neither? That's three days off work in the same week!"

"I know," I chuckled. "You should spend the holiday with your family. And you can take advantage of some of the Black Friday sales."

"It'll be the first Black Friday I got off work in five years."

"And it's about time. I'm sure you'll enjoy it."

"Oh, I sure enough will. What do you and Eugene have planned for the holiday?"

"Nothing special. Some of our friends invited us over. But because of my medical situation, we decided it'd be better to stay home this year and have a quiet celebration alone. With relatives coming for Christmas, we have so much shopping and cooking to do, I need to save my energy for that."

"I'll include you in my prayers. I been doing a lot of that lately. Ending my relationship with Mrs. Goldstein, dealing with Cynthia's antics, and this mess about us moving makes my head spin like a whirlybird. You giving me the rest of this week off would be like a shot in the arm. But you don't have to do that."

"I insist. And you don't have to worry. You'll still get paid for those days."

"Thank you, Rosemary," Ethel said with a sigh of relief. "I didn't want to bring that up, but I can't tell you how much I appreciate knowing that my pay won't be shy for this week. Now I can relax and really enjoy the holiday."

"Ethel, I don't want to make things any harder for you. Not only do I appreciate your help, I enjoy your company."

"And I enjoy yours too." Ethel looked out the window again. "I see it's done stopped raining. If you don't mind, can I leave a little early today before it starts back up? Sometimes when the weather is messy, the buses is late. If I miss one of my transfers, it could take me twice as long to get home. And I don't want to spend no money on cabs."

My breath caught in my throat. "Oh! Ethel, I'd be glad to drive you home today. As a matter of fact, I could drive you home every day for as long as you're here. I'm sorry I hadn't thought of doing that before now."

"I hope you don't think I was hinting for you to start driving me home."

"I know you weren't. But I won't take no for an answer," I said sharply, already rising from the couch. "I'd love to meet the kids, if you don't mind."

Ethel's face lit up. "I'm sure glad to hear that. I brag so much about y'all and your beautiful house, they done asked me half a dozen times when they could meet y'all."

"I don't know when they can meet Eugene, but they can meet me today."

I wished I hadn't called up Eugene to let him know that I was going to drive Ethel home.

"Baby, I don't think that's a good idea. You don't need to overexert yourself," he said in a stern tone.

I hadn't wanted Ethel to hear what I said, so I had called him up from the kitchen landline. "Driving won't overexert me. And Inglewood is not that far from here. Even in heavy traffic, I could make it there and back in twenty or thirty minutes," I protested. "Besides, I feel much better than I felt last week."

"You're feeling better because you've been taking it easy. Why don't you have Uber or Lyft take her home? I don't think you should be doing too much driving again yet. Traffic is pretty bad this time of day and there are a lot of volatile drivers on the road. Especially in this nasty weather. If she's willing to wait until I get home, I'd be happy to drive her."

"I'm sure she wouldn't mind waiting. But I'm anxious to get out of the house now, and I'd love to meet her great-grandchildren."

"All right. Give me a call the minute you get to her place, and when you get back home."

"I will," I said. And then I turned my cell phone off before I put it in my purse.

CHAPTER 15

Ethel lived in a two-story white-stucco apartment building, with four units, located on a street with a lot of older houses and other apartment buildings that resembled hers. I was surprised and pleased to see how well-kept most of them looked. "That's the store I work at on Saturdays," she said, pointing to a small convenience store at the end of the block.

"This looks like a very nice neighborhood," I commented, parking in front of her building behind a coffee-colored minivan.

"It is, but it ain't nowhere near as nice as yours. Me and the kids love it, anyway, because we feel safe here."

Before I could speak again, she opened the door and piled out of the car. I was glad to see she lived in a secure building. She removed her keys from her purse, and just as she was about to open the door to the lobby, someone buzzed us in. We got out of the rickety elevator on the second floor.

"Granny, how come you home so early?" a cute, thin preteen boy asked when we entered the living room.

"Mrs. Johnson gave me a ride home," Ethel said with a smile as she embraced the boy. "This is Anthony," she introduced. "Son, this is the nice lady I work for."

"Hi," he muttered shyly.

"Cynthia, Eddie, I'm home!" Ethel yelled. She removed her coat and waved me to a metal folding chair facing a shabby brown sofa. "Rosemary, let me have your coat." She hung hers and mine on a rack by the front door.

Eddie, who looked almost enough like his brother to be his twin, galloped into the room and stopped in front of Ethel. He screwed up his face when she tickled his chin. "Granny, Cynthia drank up all the Gatorade," he complained, looking from Ethel to me.

"There's a fresh bottle in the pantry," Ethel said gently.

Seconds later, a cute teenage girl, with shoulder-length dyed-red hair in braids, shuffled into the room with a sullen look on her face.

"Cynthia, Eddie, this is Mrs. Johnson. I used to take care of her husband when he was a young boy."

"You already told us that," Cynthia said in a flat tone. She flopped down on the arm of the couch with her arms folded. She wore a light blue denim dress and her medium-length nails had a rose design on each one. "Hi, Miss Rosemary," she muttered, giving me a brief glance. Then she immediately turned her attention to Ethel. "Can I go to Ciara's house and eat dinner with them this evening?"

"You had dinner with them yesterday, sweet pea. You're eating with your family today," Ethel replied, giving her a stern look.

"But they're having gumbo!" Cynthia hollered.

"We're having gumbo this evening too," Ethel said in a low but firm tone. She abruptly turned to face me. "Rosemary, would you like to stay and have dinner with us?"

"Oh no," I said, holding up my hand. "Some other time would be nice though. And if you don't mind, I'd like to bring Eugene with me."

"Me and the kids would love that. I'm sure that after all the lunches and dinners Eugene eats in restaurants with them stars he works with, he'd like a home-cooked meal with regular folks every now and then," Ethel said, beaming. "Kids, there is pictures of a bunch of famous folks on the walls in Rosemary's house. They even been to their house for cookouts and whatnot."

"Can we . . . um . . . c-can we meet some of those stars?" Anthony stammered.

I could tell from his low-pitched tone, and the way he was fidgeting, that he was shy. When I looked at him, he blinked and bit his bottom lip.

"Maybe two or three when they're not too busy," he added. He was so precious, I wanted to scoop him up and cradle him in my arms. Even though he was almost as tall as I was.

"The next time we have a cookout with some of the stars we know, you're all invited," I replied.

"Granny said y'all got a pool," Eddie said. His piercing black eyes sparkled like diamonds. His tone was loud and firm.

"Yes, we do have a pool. It's nothing fancy or as big as some of our neighbors, but you're welcome to come over and use it when the weather gets warmer," I said.

"What about me?" Cynthia asked.

"You're all welcome," I answered, smiling. "Cynthia, I love the design on your nails."

"I just got them done yesterday and the polish is already peeling," she griped.

"What do you expect from the cheap nail salons you go to?" Eddie teased.

"I own a nail salon in Beverly Hills. When I return to work, you're welcome to come in and get yours done, on the house."

"For real?" Cynthia gasped. She finally smiled.

"For real," I replied, chuckling.

"Rosemary, I know you already told me that you and Eugene plan on spending Thanksgiving alone. We would love to have y'all join us," Ethel said with a twinkle in her eye. "You know how much I enjoy you and Eugene's company."

"We enjoy your company too. And thank you for

the invitation, but that's all right," I said with both hands in the air.

"I'm cooking the sweet potato pies and dressing. You want me to bring you and your husband a plate? I have a bus pass," Cynthia said. She had a pleading look on her face. She didn't seem nearly as "obnoxious" as Ethel seemed to think she was. At least, not to me. And she was not nearly as "bratty" as some of the young trust-funders who came to the salon.

"Girl, you just want to see that pool!" Anthony accused, making a face at his sister. Maybe he wasn't as shy as I thought a few moments ago.

"Miss Rosemary, I wish you and your husband would come over tomorrow so we can meet him," Eddie tossed in.

"Honey, Mrs. Johnson say she's going to spend Thanksgiving alone with her husband," Ethel said. "Rosemary, I'll fix some leftovers and bring them with me when I come on Monday. I always cook more food than we can eat."

I swallowed hard and held my breath. "That's all right, Ethel. If it really means that much to you, Eugene and I would love to come have Thanksgiving dinner with you and your family."

"You have no idea how much it means to me," Ethel replied, giving me a look of adoration.

The boys started talking about how much they liked school and even what their plans were when they graduated. Eddie announced that he was going to be a baker when he grew up. His eyes almost popped out of his head when I told him that my parents had owned a catering business. Anthony wanted to be a policeman so he could get rid of people like the ones who had killed his mother and grandmother. At intervals Cynthia muttered a few comments about how "lame" her brothers were for dreaming so big. But at least she was part of the conversation. Even after the kids left the room, I was still enjoying myself so much, I lost track of time.

"Rosemary, I hope we ain't keeping you from nothing important," Ethel said, sitting on her lumpy couch while sipping Gatorade. She had gotten up a few times to use the bathroom. I hadn't budged from the metal chair I'd been sitting in the whole time.

"Not at all," I said, waving my hand. "I love hearing about your 'down South' adventures. They remind me of some of the ones my parents used to share."

"Well, I wouldn't exactly call them 'adventures,' or anything near like that. Life was rough for us during the days before integration. I remember one day when me and my sister Carlene went to town with my uncle Wally. He needed to buy some tools, so we went in a hardware store next door to a restaurant. While he was busy talking to the clerk, me and Carlene wandered out the door and into the restaurant. I was only five years old and she was four, so neither one of us could read yet. That's why we didn't know what was on the sign posted in the front window, and on the wall above the counter inside. A great big old bulldog of a white man came running up to us with the meanest look on his face I ever seen. He was yelling and screaming bloody murder and asking how come we had ignored the sign that said, 'White Folks Only.' When we told him we couldn't read, he read it to us. He got even madder and said he wasn't surprised because folks like us—he called us a word I never use, but it starts with the letter n—was too dumb to learn. Next thing I knew, he threatened to call the police. Me and my sister took off running as fast as we could out the door. We never went back in that hardware store."

"That must have been so traumatic," I said with a shudder.

"Sure enough. To this day I get nervous when I go in a restaurant run by white folks. But you know, I've known some of the nicest white folks ever, even back in Bugtussle, Kentucky. They outnumber the bad ones a hundred, maybe even a thousand, to one. That's why it don't make no sense for me to complain."

"That's a good way of looking at things. Despite what you've been through, I'm glad you still have such a positive outlook on life, Ethel."

"Well, it's because the Lord always put the right people in my path when I need them the most." Ethel sniffed and looked at me for a few moments before she continued. "Um, you serious about us coming to stay with you and Eugene until we find a place?"

"Yes, I am serious," I said firmly.

"That's the nicest and most generous thing anybody ever offered me. I been thinking about it ever since you told me. It's one of the things that's been helping me smile these days."

"I want you to keep smiling."

CHAPTER 16

It was seven p.m. when I left Ethel's apartment and returned to my car. As soon as I sat down, I took my cell phone out of my purse and checked my messages. Min-jee had sent a text. Genelle had left two voice mail messages, and Eugene had left three voice mails and two texts. Each one had asked where I was. I decided not to return any calls, but I texted Min-jee and Genelle to let them know I'd taken Ethel home and would call them later. I'd be seeing Eugene soon enough.

Within minutes after I drove away from Ethel's place, it started raining again. And much harder than it had earlier in the day. That slowed me down considerably, so it took longer for me to get back to my neighborhood.

When I made it to our driveway, Eugene was in the living room. He was peeping out the front window, with his hand shading his eyes. There was a wild-eyed look on his face when I got inside.

"Where in the world have you been, Rosemary?"

"I drove Ethel home," I said, removing my coat. "I told you that when I called you this afternoon. Remember?"

"And I told you that I don't think you should be out driving just yet. If I had known that you were going to be roaming around at night in the rain, I would have left my office early and taken Ethel home myself," he said in a gruff tone as he followed me to the couch. We sat down at the same time.

"I drove to Inglewood, not Mexico," I protested.

"Is that where you've been all this time?" he yelled.

"Of course," I shot back. "I told you I wanted to meet the kids." I sighed and gave him a misty-eyed look. Just thinking about Eddie, Anthony, and Cynthia made me feel so blissful, there was nothing Eugene could say that would upset me. "Baby, they are so cute. I wish I could have stayed longer."

" 'Longer'? Several hours weren't enough? If you had stayed *longer,* I would have called the cops and reported you as a missing person."

I rolled my eyes and neck at the same time. "Stop overreacting, sweetie." I briefly massaged the top of his head. That always tamed him.

"I'm glad you enjoyed your visit," he said in a much softer tone. "But, as long as you're still under a doctor's care, don't you go off like that again. If you had called me when you got to Ethel's, like you said you would, I would have felt better. And if you had called to let me know you were going to stay there for a while, I would have felt even better." Eugene caressed the side of my face, puckered his lips, and gave me a peck on my cheek.

"I'm sorry, sugar. It won't happen again. Happy now?"

"I guess." Eugene studied my face and finally gave me a smile. "I'll let it slide this time. Meeting those kids must have lifted your spirits. You seem almost slaphappy. You were a little down in the dumps before I left the house this morning. There was such a puppy-dog look on your face, I was surprised you didn't bark."

We laughed.

"I didn't think I was 'down in the dumps' enough for you to notice. And I certainly don't have a 'puppy-dog' face now. And I know it's because meeting those kids was so uplifting. That was one thing. I also enjoyed listening to more of Ethel's stories about what it was like when she was growing up in Kentucky. You should have heard some of the things she told me."

"I've probably already heard some of the same ones," Eugene said with a snicker. "She used to tell Lawrence and me all kinds of anecdotes when she was trying to make a point. I can't tell you how many times she told us we didn't know how lucky we were compared to what she went through growing up. At the end of the day, she still turned out okay. That's all that matters."

"That's so true. For a woman who didn't finish high school, she is one of the wisest and most optimistic people I ever met. I could listen to her stories every day. I can't wait to hear more." I paused and exhaled. "And she's so compassionate. She actually forgave the man who killed her granddaughter."

"Oh? She knew him?"

I nodded. "He was a friend of the family. He's turned his life completely around, but he'll be spending the rest of it in prison." I shook my head. "Enough about that gloomy subject!" I exclaimed. "Anyway, I really enjoyed visiting Ethel's home."

"Did you bring up the subject of her moving in with us? I hope you didn't. We need to think it through a little more."

"No, I didn't bring it up. I still think we should pursue it though. Ethel seemed a little more receptive about it today than she did the first time we discussed it."

"What?" Eugene struggled for air and narrowed his eyes. "You just said you didn't bring that up today."

"I didn't. But she did. All she wanted to know was if I was serious about moving them in with us until they find a place. I told her I was. And if you don't mind, I'm going to invite her and the children to join us for Christmas dinner. I'm sure Lawrence would love to see Ethel again after all these years."

"Lawrence and his crew won't be coming for Christmas."

"Why not? I promised his kids we'd visit Knott's Berry Farm again. They were really looking forward to it."

"I was too. But we can always go the next time they visit. The thing is, Lena's mother had a stroke two nights ago. Lawrence called me this evening just before I left my office. That's one of the messages I left for you this evening."

"Oh no! Is she going to be all right?"

"She's not doing so well, and the prognosis is not good."

I suddenly felt overwhelmingly sad. What I was going through with my health was bad, but not nearly as critical as a stroke. I rubbed the back of my head. The news Eugene had just reported had made it throb all of a sudden. On top of that, my chest felt like somebody was sitting on it. "Did he say if it was a massive stroke?"

"He didn't say, but it must have been. Yesterday she could still move about. Today she can't move or talk."

"We have to go—"

Eugene shook his head and frowned. "Rosemary, you haven't fully recovered yet. With the weather in Connecticut being so brutal now, traveling is out of the question for you."

"Poor Lena. She and her mother are so close. And she just lost her father last year."

"Lawrence will keep us posted."

"Good. I'll give him and Lena a call tomorrow."

Despite the bleak news about Lawrence's mother-in-law, I felt the joy of the day coming back to me. "Eugene, Ethel's kids are absolutely adorable, especially the boys. Cynthia was a little aloof and testy, but she's a teenager. Her demeanor got better before I left. Anyway, I can't wait for you to meet them."

"I can't wait to meet them too."

"I'm glad to hear that. You'll meet them the day after tomorrow. We're having Thanksgiving dinner at Ethel's house."

CHAPTER 17

Eugene reared back and looked at me with his mouth hanging open. "You told Ethel we'd eat Thanksgiving dinner at her house? I wish you had checked with me before you made that decision," he said in a serious tone. "Several folks invited us to join them for the holiday so you wouldn't have to tire yourself out cooking. And we'd discussed going to a nice restaurant for Thanksgiving, Ro."

"I don't want to spend the holiday with any of our friends. I'm not ready to answer a bunch of their questions about my health. And I know we did talk about going to a restaurant, but it's probably too late to get a reservation at any of the places we like. I'd rather have a home-cooked meal anyway."

"If that's the case, I'll cook."

"No, you won't. As hard as you've been working these past few weeks, you deserve a break. Baby, you should have seen how Ethel's and those kids' faces lit up when I told her we'd be coming over on Thursday.

But if you really don't want to go, I'll call her first thing in the morning and cancel—"

Eugene snorted loudly and gave me a hot look. "No, don't do that. We'll go. But, even though I sound like a broken record, in the future, before you make decisions about anything that concerns both of us, run it by me first, okay?"

"Okay." I stood up and rubbed the top of his bald head. "Hmm. Your noggin is not as hard as it looks."

I stirred around more than I should have. It wasn't long before I was aching in a couple of places, and I felt a bit nauseous. An hour after I'd eaten only half of the steak Eugene had grilled, I returned to the living-room couch and fell asleep. I didn't wake up until ten o'clock on Wednesday morning. I sat up in bed, surprised to see Eugene hovering over me. "I don't remember coming to bed."

"You didn't. You fell asleep on the living-room couch and I carried you up here last night."

"Oh. I guess I was really tired, huh?"

"Apparently. After you stopped mauling my head, you asked me to go into the library and pick out a couple of videos for us to watch. By the time I returned, five or six minutes later, you were dead to the world."

"I was."

"Yes, and that worries me. I don't want you to do much of anything today."

"I won't." I rubbed my stomach. It was still a little swollen, but there was very little soreness now. But my legs felt crampy, and there was a mild pain in my lower back. I decided not to tell Eugene any of that though. "Why are you still in your pajamas?" I glanced at the clock on the nightstand. "Aren't you going to work?"

"Since you gave Ethel today off, I decided to work from home today and I'm taking Friday off too. I'm going to borrow Randy's boat to go fishing for a few hours Friday morning."

I gave Eugene an incredulous look. "You said you didn't want to go by yourself!" I exclaimed.

"I'll find somebody. I wish you'd change your mind about joining me. It would be nice for you to get out in some fresh air for a little while."

"I'd rather be cooped up in the house than cooped up on a boat out in the middle of the open water."

"If I do go, I won't stay long. I just don't want to leave you alone. Maybe I can get Professor Daley from next door to come keep you company until I get back."

"Don't you dare bother her. I'll be fine for a few hours. Besides, Genelle is coming over after she finishes her Black Friday shopping. And wait a minute! Don't you have another meeting with that fussy soap opera actress on Friday?"

"I sent her a text and told her I couldn't see her until Monday morning."

"Humph. I'm sure she didn't want to hear that." I cleared my throat and sat up straighter.

"She didn't. She sent me a strongly worded text back to let me know she'd have to miss her Pilates class to meet with me on Monday." He chuckled.

"What did you say to her about that?"

"I told her that if she can't meet with me then, she'd have to wait another week, because I have appointments booked back-to-back every other day. Don't worry about her. I'm not. You're my focus today. And I want you to know now that you don't even have to get up today."

"Eugene, I don't want to stay in bed all day. Anyway, I'm doing a lot better than I was last week."

"You'll be doing even better if you stay off your feet today. I didn't mention it, but you didn't look good at all last night. And you were as limp as a wet noodle when I lifted you off the couch and brought you upstairs. Now stay put and I'll fix breakfast."

I drank two cups of coffee and ate some oatmeal in bed. But just before noon, I got out of bed anyway. After I hobbled to the bathroom and took a shower, I joined Eugene on the living-room couch. I had put on a dress, but he was still in his pajamas. We watched a few game shows on TV and returned a few phone calls during commercial breaks. When the landline on the end table rang during the next commercial, I grabbed it. I was thrilled to see my brother-in-law's name on the caller ID.

"Lawrence!" I hollered, beckoning for Eugene to move closer. I punched the speaker feature. "Eugene is here."

"I know. I just spoke to his secretary and she told me he'd be working from home today," Lawrence replied.

"How is Lena's mom?" Eugene asked.

"She's still in pretty bad shape. Poor Lena is worried sick."

"I'm so sorry to hear that. I'll pray for her. Tell the kids they can visit us on their spring break," I threw in. "I know how excited they were to come out here next month. And I hope you and Lena can take off work and come with them. Let her know I'll order tickets for us to attend a taping of *Let's Make a Deal* and *Dr. Phil,* if they're taping that week. She had a ball at the tapings the last time we went."

"I'll let her know that."

"Where are you now, bro?" Eugene asked.

"I'm at home. We spent the night at the hospital. Lena wanted to be close by, in case Mama Briley woke up," Lawrence said with his voice cracking.

"And there's been no improvement?" I asked.

"None at all."

"Lawrence, let Lena know we're praying for her mother," I added.

"Thanks, Ro. Well, I just wanted to check in with you two. I need to go get some rest myself now."

After we hung up, I rested my head on Eugene's

shoulder and sobbed for a few minutes until I fell asleep. When I woke up, it was dark outside. And I was back in the bed, with Eugene hovering over me again.

"Maybe I should call Ethel and let her know we won't be able to make it tomorrow," he said gently.

"You'll do no such thing!"

"Baby, you can't even stay awake for more than a few hours at a time. Do you think Ethel would want you to come to her house if she knew that?"

"Maybe she wouldn't. But she'd probably insist on coming over here to look after me. Now we're going to eat dinner with her and those children tomorrow. I promise we won't stay more than an hour or two."

CHAPTER 18

Eugene and I spent part of Thanksgiving morning calling up friends and relatives in various parts of the country to wish them a happy holiday.

Ethel had told us to come over at four p.m., but we got there twenty minutes earlier. She greeted us with so much enthusiasm, you would have thought she hadn't seen us in weeks. "Lord, Lord, Lord! I'm so glad y'all made it!" she hollered. After giving us bear hugs and kisses on our cheeks, she hung our coats on the rack by the front door. Then she steered us into the kitchen, where she had already set the table.

I was amazed to see such a bright white linen tablecloth. I couldn't remember the last time I'd seen so much food in one place. In addition to a turkey and a rump roast on the table, there was a huge bowl of corn bread dressing, two platters of sliced ham, three bowls of various vegetables, a dozen rolls, and three gallon-size pitchers of lemonade.

"We like to eat on time, so y'all take a seat and we

can get started while everything is still nice and hot," Ethel said.

"Where are the children?" I asked, looking around. Just then, Eddie and Anthony galloped into the room, grinning from ear to ear. Their curly black hair looked like it had been recently cut. They were dressed in crisp white shirts with bow ties and dark pants. Cynthia, wearing a dingy white T-shirt, skinny jeans, and a baseball cap turned backward, trailed behind them. Her nose and forehead were scrunched up, one eyebrow was higher than the other, and her lips were pursed. You would have thought she was about to get a whupping.

"Cynthia, sugar, ain't you going to dress for dinner?" Ethel asked in a gentle tone. There was a smile on her face.

"I am dressed for dinner," Cynthia said in a low, whiny tone.

Ethel rolled her eyes and shook her head, and the boys snickered. "Kids, where is y'all's manners at?" Ethel asked, clapping her hands. "Show some respect to our company. This is Rosemary's husband, Eugene."

"Hello, sir," Eddie chirped, looking from me to Eugene as he plopped down in a chair next to Ethel.

Cynthia took a seat next to me. "Nice to meet you, Mr. Eugene," she mumbled in such a low tone, I was probably the only one who could hear her. She kept her head down and her lips pressed together as if she thought words she didn't want to release would spill out.

"Mr. Eugene, Miss Rosemary said you like to fish," Anthony piped up, flopping down in the chair across from his brother.

"I sure do. I'm going to go out again soon," Eugene said.

"Where at?" Anthony asked.

"Malibu Pier. A friend of mine has a boat he lets me borrow."

"Ooh-wee!" Eddie exclaimed. "Our grandfather rented a boat one day and took us fishing."

"Did you enjoy it?" Eugene asked.

"Uh-huh. It was the most fun we ever had. Grandpa had planned to take us to Disneyland that same weekend, until he found out how much the tickets cost to get in. He borrowed a boat from the man he used to work for, and we went fishing instead."

"Did you catch any fish?" I asked.

"Yup, but not that many. Just one white sea bass and a couple of mackerels. We were going to go the following weekend too. But Grandpa didn't live that long."

"I'm sorry to hear that," I muttered.

"Well, if it's all right with you, Ethel, maybe the boys can go with me the next time I decide to go," Eugene blurted out, glancing at me from the corner of his eye. I smiled and gave him a nod. "Uh, I was thinking about going tomorrow morning."

"I don't see why not," Ethel replied. "So long as they have their chores and homework done."

Eddie and Anthony whooped and hollered until Ethel made them stop. She cleared her throat, tapped the side of her glass with a spoon, and said, "I'd like to say grace, and if anybody else wants to add something before we eat, please do so." She closed her eyes and cupped her hands in prayer. Everybody except Cynthia did the same. "Lord, bless this food and thank You for leading me and my babies to Eugene and Rosemary. Amen."

Right after we opened our eyes, Eugene spoke. "I praise the Lord for reuniting me with Ethel. And I thank Him for continuing to bless Rosemary and me so abundantly. We have a lot of material things to be thankful for. I am even more grateful that Rosemary's health is getting better by the day, and that we have so many good people in our lives." He paused and looked at me, then around the table. "I hope you'll all be in our lives for a long time to come."

"I hope so too," Ethel mumbled. She paused and made a sweeping gesture around the table. "Now I done cooked up a storm. I want everybody to eat like hogs."

"Granny said we might move in with y'all," Eddie blurted out.

"What?" Cynthia gasped.

Eugene gasped too. When he looked at me from the corner of his eye, I didn't know what to expect him to say next. Luckily, he said just what I wanted to hear. "Rosemary and I discussed the housing dilemma you all are facing. We have enough room for everybody at this table."

"Not me!" Cynthia hollered. "I don't want to change schools and have to make new friends all over again."

"Rosemary, I told the boys what me and you talked about already. I hadn't told Cynthia yet," Ethel said, giving me an apologetic look. She sucked in some air and looked at her great-granddaughter. "Honey, things are going to change, now that our building has been sold. I been advised that the new owner wants to move his daughter into our apartment because it's the biggest one and got the best view, and almost-new appliances," she said in a gentle tone. "Rosemary and Eugene will let us stay with them temporarily until I save up enough to cover moving expenses."

"Temporary or not, I don't care. I said that I am not changing schools and giving up my friends!" Cynthia pushed her chair away from the table, jumped up, and ran out of the room. Ethel trotted behind her.

The silence that followed was deafening. Eugene shifted in his seat; I cleared my throat. Nobody else moved a muscle until Eddie asked impatiently, "Can we eat already?"

"Let's wait until Ethel and Cynthia return," I suggested.

"Cynthia is going to run away again," Anthony said, shaking his head. He looked at me with a woeful expression on his face. "Every time she gets mad, she runs away. But she never runs too far. Just down the street to Ciara Weatherspoon's house. That's her best friend."

"And when she don't run away, she mouths off," Eddie added.

In spite of all the good food in front of us, eating was the last thing on my mind. I had lost my appetite. Two minutes later, Ethel shuffled back to the kitchen alone, looking like she wanted to crawl into a hole. I didn't want to add to her misery, so I started eating like a hog.

We ate in silence for the first few minutes, but then Eugene got the conversation going again. "Ethel, I want you to know that no matter what happens, you can count on us to be there for you and the children."

"What about Cynthia?" Eddie asked.

"That includes Cynthia," I said quickly, making myself sound as cheerful and hopeful as possible. "I'm sure she'll eventually come around."

"I sure hope so, Rosemary." Ethel blinked back a tear that had formed in the corner of her eye. "I sure hope so," she repeated with her voice cracking.

When we finished eating, Eugene, Ethel, and I went into the living room. Eddie and Anthony stayed in the kitchen to clean up and put the leftovers away, which was part of their daily routine. Ethel sat in the La-Z-Boy chair facing Eugene and me on the couch. "I want to apologize for Cynthia's behavior. I don't know why she'd want to disrespect nice people like y'all," Ethel said.

"You don't need to apologize," I assured her. "We didn't feel disrespected."

"Y'all might not think so, but other folks would," Ethel said.

Eugene and I looked at each other and then at Ethel. "Let's not worry about that for the time being. But we want you to know that no matter what happens, our door is open, and Cynthia will always be welcome," I said firmly, looking at Eugene as I spoke. I was glad to see the look of approval on his face.

CHAPTER 19

Half an hour had passed since we'd finished eating and Cynthia was still holed up in the bedroom she shared with Ethel. I was surprised to see her when I went to use the bathroom. We collided in the narrow hallway as I was coming out. "I'm sorry," I said, backing away from her.

She gave me a blank stare before she spoke. "Um, were you serious about letting me come to your salon to get my nails done?"

"Of course," I said quickly. "I'll do them myself. If you want them done before I return to work in January, I'd even be willing to make a house call."

"A house call? For real?"

"Yes. We have several clients who like to get their nails done in the comfort of their own homes."

"People do that?"

"Some people."

"Oh yeah!" She snickered and rolled her eyes. "I

keep forgetting that you real rich people don't live the way the rest of us do."

"I don't know about that. And for your information, Eugene and I are not 'real rich people.'"

"Then how can y'all afford to pay Granny and live in that big house with a swimming pool that she's always bragging about?"

"Well, we make very good money and we don't live extravagantly. Believe it or not, I still shop at Walmart, Target, and all the other discount stores," I admitted.

"You do?" Cynthia's eyes got so big, it looked like they were about to pop out of their sockets. "You roll up to Walmart in that big SUV I saw you and Mr. Eugene park in front of our building?"

"That's Eugene's car. I drive a Lexus."

"A Lexus," she repeated with a dreamy look in her eyes.

"I have three more years to go before I pay it off in full. When I do, I'm going to drive it until it falls apart. Then I'll get a Honda or some other economy car."

It warmed my heart to hear Cynthia laugh. "I think it's so cool that you and Mr. Eugene don't like to flaunt your wealth."

"That's for sure. But we like to share as much of it as we can with people who need some assistance."

"Yeah. Granny told us how much you pay her for doing almost nothing," Cynthia chuckled again.

"Nothing? Pfffttt!" I waved my hand. "Well, she does a whole lot of 'nothing.' She helps me bathe, fixes my lunch, and spends time doing all sorts of chores around the house. Some days she insists on cooking breakfast and dinner, even though it's not part of her job."

"I'm just happy you let her come work for you until you get well. But"—Cynthia paused and gave me a look that was so sad, I was surprised she didn't burst into tears—"she is a real old lady, so don't work her too hard. I don't know what we'd do if something happened to her."

"Honey, you shouldn't worry about things like that."

"I know, but I can't help it. I hope she lives long enough to see all three of us finish high school. When I graduate, I'm going to get a job right away and take care of her, and she'll never have to work again." When she stopped talking, there was a dreamy look in her eyes for a couple of seconds. "If it takes too long for me to find a good job, or a good husband, I'm going to join the military and send the money they give me home to Granny. I'd rather get married though—but only to a man who'll promise me that he'll help me take care of her. I want a husband like yours. Granny's told us so much about him and what a big shot he is. But men like him only go for special ladies like you . . ."

I had to blink hard to hold back my tears. "There is nothing 'special' about me, Cynthia. Just be the best person you can possibly be, and the best man, and everything else good, will come to you."

Cynthia giggled. "I hope you're right. Anyway, it was nice meeting your husband. I'm glad you and he came today. It made Granny so happy. She'll be bragging to her friends about it for days. Just like she did that first day after she got home from her interview with you." Cynthia started shifting her weight from one foot to the other and blinking nervously. Something told me she wanted to keep talking.

"Why don't we go into the living room with everybody else?" I suggested.

"Um, I'll do that later. I'll call you when I'm ready to come get my nails done." She whirled around and disappeared into the bathroom before I could say another word.

When I returned to the living room, Eugene was sitting cross-legged on the floor between Anthony and Eddie, tinkering with a flip cell phone and talking about their upcoming fishing trip tomorrow.

Ethel stood in the middle of the floor with her hands on her hips. "That phone done seen its last days," she commented.

"Everybody else got smartphones!" Anthony griped, giving Ethel a hopeful look.

"Everybody else got smartphone money too," Ethel

pointed out. She looked at me, rolled her eyes, and shook her head. "Mrs. Goldstein owns an ePhone that she paid almost a thousand dollars for. Whew!"

"It's iPhone, not ePhone, Granny," Eddie corrected with a snicker.

"Whatever it's called, we ain't got that kind of money to buy one," she insisted.

"Boys, I hate to tell you, but it's time to lay this phone to rest," Eugene said as he wobbled up off the floor. "It has no dial tone and the buttons stick. It's time to replace it."

"Maybe Santa Claus will bring a couple of smart-phones next month and . . ." I stopped talking when Eddie and Anthony stifled their snickers.

I looked at Eugene. He winked and said, "Santa Claus always came through for me." He winked at the boys and they started grinning like the Cheshire cat.

Ten minutes later, Eugene and I left. As soon as we got into his SUV, I hauled off and kissed him.

"What was that for?" he asked.

"For you being you, *Mr. Claus*," I answered.

"Giving the boys new phones for Christmas is the least I can do," Eugene replied as he started the motor. "Well, it doesn't look like your plan to have Ethel and the kids come stay with us is going to pan out. If Cynthia refuses to come, Ethel will probably give in and move in with her relatives in South Central."

"If it comes to that, Cynthia would still have to change schools and make new friends."

"I don't know what else to say on this subject, Rosemary. I love Ethel like she's family. As far as I'm concerned, she is. And I already have feelings for those children. Even Cynthia. If we had some legal rights, it would—"

A thought struck me like a bolt out of the blue. I immediately interrupted Eugene. "We'll adopt them!"

"Excuse me?"

"Let's look at this from a realistic point of view. Ethel could be around for another ten or fifteen years. According to her doctor, maybe even longer than that because her health is excellent for a woman her age. She told me that she's never even had any problems with her blood pressure and cholesterol like me. But she is getting on in years. If she's not lucky enough to live well into her seventies or eighties, Lord knows what will happen to those sweet children. If we adopt them in the very near future, Ethel could relax and enjoy her golden years."

"Baby, having them move in with us on a temporary basis is one thing. Ethel might take us up on it eventually. But we know Cynthia won't go for it. With that being the case, do you honestly think *adoption* is the answer? That's a huge leap from their just staying with us for a few weeks or months."

"Eugene, I wish you'd be more optimistic. This

could be our last chance to have a family of our own," I asserted.

"I agree with you on that. But have you said anything to Ethel about adoption? I hope you haven't. The last thing I want is for you to put her in a spot that'll make her so uncomfortable, she might decide to leave before you're well enough to be on your own."

"No, I haven't said anything about adoption to her. But I will when I think the time is right."

"All right, Ro. I guess you won't change your mind, huh?"

"Nope."

CHAPTER 20

Genelle came to the house shortly after noon, right after her annual Black Friday shopping spree. This was the first year Min-jee and I had not accompanied her. Min-jee and her family had gone to San Diego on Wednesday evening to celebrate Thanksgiving with some of her relatives.

After Genelle had shown me all of her purchases—mostly things she didn't need and would never use—she regaled me with hilarious accounts of frantic shoppers she'd encountered at the mall. That took at least twenty minutes. Then she flopped down in the chair across from me on the couch and gave me a wistful look.

"How was your Thanksgiving at Ethel's house, Ro?"

I took a deep breath and told her the high points. Then I added, "Ethel's building was recently sold, and it looks like she's going to have to find a new place to live. Her funds are limited, and she may not have enough money for moving expenses by the time she has to vacate. Eugene and I are going to have her and the kids move in with us."

Genelle's jaw dropped. "What did you say?" she shrieked.

"You heard me."

"Yes, I did. I'm sure Ethel is not happy about having to move. But do you think bringing them here is the right solution? What if it takes six or seven months for her to save up enough for a new place? Why don't you just lend the money to her?"

"If she asked, I'd do it without hesitation, and I know Eugene would too. But Ethel is way too proud to ask us for money. And if we offered it to her, she wouldn't accept it. She'd probably ask her church for help first. They've helped her before. If she moves in with us, she wouldn't have to pay rent. She'd be able to save the money a lot sooner."

"Well, why doesn't she go to her church for help this time instead of moving in with you and Eugene? Sharing a place is a big step, and it could be a bad one. It could ruin your friendship with her."

"Why do you say that?"

"Honey, no matter how well you know and like somebody, living with them is a whole different ball of wax. The girl I was best friends with all through junior high and high school invited me to share an apartment with her when we graduated. I thought it was a great idea at the time because we were so close. You rarely saw one of us without the other. Come to find out, we didn't know one another as well as we thought. I won't even bother telling you all the details about the problems we had. But there were so many, I'd be here all night trying to cover them all. Anyway, within a month we were at each other's throat so much, I was so anxious to get away from that girl, I packed in the middle of the night and left that place running. My best friend and I never spoke again."

I swallowed hard, and looked Genelle straight in the eyes. "I'm not worried about that happening with Ethel. Besides, I invited her to move in because her situation in general is pretty bleak."

"Oh? In what way?" Genelle leaned forward and looked at me with her eyes narrowed.

"She's worried about what'll happen to the kids when she passes."

"Oh no!" Genelle boomed with a panic-stricken expression on her face. Then she asked in a gentle tone, "Is she terminal?"

"No, she's as healthy as a horse. But she's very concerned about the kids' future in her absence. That's one reason I don't think lending her the money to move is a good idea. She'd have a new place, but she'd still be worried about what's going to happen to the kids. Therefore, we're going to offer to adopt them. If she goes for it, that'd be one less thing for her to worry about. And Ethel will have a permanent home herself with us."

Genelle's jaw dropped again. She reared back in

her seat and looked at me as if I'd lost my mind. "You're *what*? Girl, you can't be serious. You want to adopt your caregiver's great-grandchildren? That's the strangest thing I've ever heard you say!" she hollered.

"What's so 'strange' about it?" I asked, shifting in my seat.

"For one thing, it seems so out of the blue. I can understand if you were considering adopting one child, but three? And taking on the responsibility of their great-grandmother? Is Eugene okay with this?"

"Oh, he's all for it. As a matter of fact, he's out on a boat in Malibu fishing with the boys right now. He fell in love with them as fast as I did."

"But you guys barely know them. They are practically strangers to you."

"You were a stranger, until I got to know you," I pointed out.

"Don't be cute," Genelle scolded, wagging her finger in my direction. Even though there was a tight look on her face and her tone was gruff, it didn't bother me at all.

"We know that Ethel is a wonderful woman down on her luck who needs some serious help. And we want to give it to her."

"Is that why you want to adopt the kids?" Genelle folded her arms across her chest and glared at me. "Rosemary, have you really thought this through? What about Ethel's family? You told me she's got folks in South Central, Compton, and Kentucky."

"They've got enough problems and children of their own. Besides, they all live in the kind of neighborhoods Ethel worked so hard to keep the kids out of."

Genelle sighed heavily and shook her head so hard, her hair flopped. "I'll say this much, I admire you for being so charitable," she admitted, speaking in a much softer tone. "But I would hate to see you bite off more than you can chew."

"I want a family, Genelle. So does Eugene. This way we won't have to sit back and wait on an adoption agency to come through for us."

"Yes, but in the long run, you might regret it."

"In what way?" I gasped.

"In every way. You've only known Ethel less than a month! Why don't you spend a few months, or even a year, to get better acquainted with her and the kids? They may seem nice and sweet up front, but who knows what they are really like?"

"If we let the adoption agency find children for us, we'd still be taking in children we don't know anything about. At least with Ethel, Eugene has a history with her. And in just the short period of time I've known her, I can tell that she's the kind of person I'd like to keep in my life. The same goes for those children."

Genelle gave me an exasperated look and held up her hands like she was surrendering. I hoped she was, because I was not about to take her advice. "Okay.

You have my blessing. Now, I'm sure you already know, raising kids is not easy."

"So? If I had kids of my own, I'd have to deal with the same issues anyway. Just from what I've seen so far, I can tell that Ethel's burden is getting to be way too difficult for her to handle on her own much longer. The sooner she gets some assistance, the better off she'll be. So will those kids."

"Well, if you've made up your mind, it won't do me or anybody else much good to try and talk you out of it, right?"

"Right."

Genelle tilted her head to the side, sighed, and gave me a look of defeat before she went on. "I don't like it, but I'll admit that it could be the best thing that could happen to Ethel and those poor kids."

I smiled. "It could be the best thing to happen to Eugene and me too."

CHAPTER 21

When Ethel arrived on Monday, her appearance stunned me. Usually, she was always neatly dressed and well-groomed. But today her hair was askew, and the dress she had on was so wrinkled, it looked like she'd slept in it. Her eyes were red and swollen, and she didn't have on the maroon-colored lipstick she always wore. Eugene had left early because he had to be in his office to participate in a three-party conference call to London with two of his most important clients. I was glad he wasn't home, so he wouldn't see how distressed Ethel looked.

"Morning, Rosemary," she said in a hoarse voice. I led her to the living-room couch immediately. She sat down with such a loud groan, it scared me.

"You don't look too good," I said, easing down next to her.

"I don't feel too good neither. I hardly slept a wink last night," she whimpered. "I got some more bad news."

"Is it Cynthia?"

"No, not this time." Ethel blew out a long, loud breath before she continued. "Mr. Stone, my building manager, came over right after we got home from church yesterday. He told us that he'd met with the new owner on Saturday and found out he will be making changes sooner than he had planned. Instead of having three or four months to find a new place to live, we got to be out by the end of December. The new owner's daughter is in a hurry to move into the building. Mr. Stone is bringing the eviction papers to me this evening. After the boys get out of school today, they are going to go to the store where I work and pick up some boxes. We'll start packing our stuff this evening."

"I'm going to call up Eugene in a few minutes and let him know. I'll tell him that I want you and the kids to move in with us as soon as possible. Maybe as soon as next week."

"I appreciate that, Rosemary, but I can't go nowhere until I figure out what to do with my furniture. I don't think I can get that sorted out by next week. I'll need more time. And Cynthia told me straight up, she's going to stay with her best friend, Ciara Weatherspoon. She packed her stuff and headed back over there last night after Mr. Stone left. Ciara's mama, Shirley, loves Cynthia like family, so I know they'll take good care of her. I always give

Shirley a few dollars every time Cynthia holes up with them."

"You're going to allow her to move in with your neighbors? Have you called the police and reported her as a runaway?"

Ethel looked so terrified, you would have thought she'd seen a ghost. "The police? Good Lord! I can't do that. Just her running away ain't serious enough for me to involve the law. Besides, I'm scared if I do, they'll pick her up and put her in the system, and I might never see her again at all. I done lost too many loved ones already."

This news was having a devastating effect on me. I suddenly felt as tired as Ethel looked. I rubbed my chest and let out a low moan.

"Rosemary, you all right?" Ethel reached over and touched my hand, which was trembling.

"Oh, I'm fine," I muttered, pulling my hand away.

"Did you take your blood pressure medicine this morning?"

"Yes. I always take it first thing in the morning." I didn't want to admit to Ethel that even with the pills I was taking for my blood pressure, I had a feeling it was still too high. The reason I thought that was because every time I heard disturbing news, or got excited about something, my heart started beating so hard and fast, I could hear it. There was no telling how much higher my blood pressure was now. I made a mental note to reschedule the appointment I'd made to see Dr. Nash and go see him sooner.

"What about them pills you take for your cholesterol?"

"I take them later in the day when I take the other medication Dr. Miller gave me."

"Well, don't you skip nary a day. Sometimes missing one little pill can make a difference." Ethel somehow managed to smile, but I couldn't.

"I am so sorry, Ethel. Listen, there is not much you need to do today. I've already taken my bath and I can fix my own lunch. We'll spend the day watching TV and chitchatting. In the meantime you just sit here and rest. I'm going to give Eugene a call and let him know what you just told me."

Ethel held up her hand. "Rosemary, I don't want to drag him into this mess too soon. He's been so nice to the boys. I can't believe he spent most of last Friday with them out on that fishing boat and treating them to dinner at a fancy restaurant in Bel Air."

"That's because he cares about those children as much as I do. He needs to know each new development as soon as possible." I blew out a loud breath and rubbed my chest again. "You can put your furniture in storage. I'll pay for it."

"Thank you, but let's put that on the back burner for a day or two. I need to get my bearings back up and running so I can focus on other things too." Ethel coughed. "This is going to be the most miserable

Christmas we ever had. My freezer went on the blink last night. If I buy a turkey, I ain't got nowhere to keep it until Christmas. Not that I plan on doing much cooking anyway."

"You won't have to. Eugene and I want you and the kids to eat Christmas dinner with us. You can help me with the cooking," I said.

"Oh, I couldn't—"

"I won't take no for an answer." I stood up and started backing out of the room. "Now you sit there and rest while I go fix us some coffee."

As soon as I got to the kitchen, I picked up the landline and called Eugene's office. I expected his secretary to tell me he was unavailable. But much to my surprise, he wasn't. He listened patiently as I told him the latest news about Ethel.

"Rosemary, I'm going to do all I can to help. If she takes us up on our offer to let her and the kids move in, that's fine with me. It's just that . . ."

Eugene's sudden hesitation worried me. "It's 'just that' what?"

"If we move Ethel and the boys in with us, that'll only solve part of her problem. She'll still have to figure out what to do about Cynthia."

"I realize that. But at least she'd be able to focus more on Cynthia and not sit around worrying about being homeless too."

There was a long moment of silence. And then I chuckled.

"What's so funny, Rosemary?"

"I was just thinking how ironic it is that we hired Ethel to assist me, and we end up assisting her."

"Ethel was a very important person to my family. I'm sure my folks would be delighted to know she's back in my life."

"I only wish it was under more pleasant circumstances," I said with a sigh.

"So do I. Look, honey, I'd love to continue this conversation. But I need to be in court in a few minutes. We'll discuss this more when I get home. Just let Ethel know she has nothing to worry about."

When I returned to the living room, Ethel had fallen asleep on the couch. She looked so small and sad, it broke my heart. I hobbled upstairs and got a blanket from the linen closet and covered her up.

She slept for the next three hours.

When Ethel woke up, it was afternoon. She sat up so abruptly, she almost slid to the floor. She gulped when she saw me sitting in the chair across from her. "Lord! I'm so sorry. I guess I was more tired than I thought. How long I been sleeping?" she asked, looking around the room.

"Not too long," I said with a warm smile. "You can sleep a little longer if you need to."

"Uh-uh. All this sleeping on the job ain't like me! I better get my tail in gear." She wiped beads of sweat off her face with her hand and lowered her tone. "What do you want me to fix for lunch? You still got any of that Thanksgiving turkey that I sent home with y'all after our dinner last week? If so, I can make a salad or some sandwiches."

"Pffftt. We finished off that turkey before we went to bed Thursday night. I made us some ham and cheese sandwiches a little while ago. Would you like coffee or tea with yours?"

Ethel ignored my question. She cleared her throat and wiped drool from her chin. "I am so ashamed of myself. I am so embarrassed."

"Why? You have no reason to be," I assured her. "You haven't done anything wrong."

"Except sleeping when I'm supposed to be working. This is the second time I done this here. I only done it one time when I was working for Mrs. Goldstein. Cynthia had gone to the store to get a bottle of pop right after dinner one evening. By midnight she hadn't come home. Even after her friend Ciara called and told me she was over there, I couldn't go to sleep. But I still got up a few hours later and went to work. Around ten o'clock that morning, I dozed off on Mrs. Goldstein's bed right after I'd made it. She didn't catch me, praise the Lord. As nice a woman as she was, she didn't tolerate none of her servants slacking off. I know that if she had caught me sleeping, she would have blessed me out. I thank you for not doing that." Ethel sniffed and rubbed her nose. "Did you talk to Eugene yet?"

"Yes, and when I speak to him again, I'm going to

ask him to arrange to have your furniture put into a storage facility when you're ready."

"That would be a big help," Ethel said with a sigh of relief. "Now you listen, I want you to know up front that we ain't going to do nothing to upset you and Eugene after we move in. I'll make sure the boys behave and clean up after themselves. Y'all won't regret helping us out, I promise. And we'll be out of your hair as soon as we find a new place."

I had given a lot of thought to what I was going to say next. But I still had trouble getting the words out. "Uh . . . there is something else I want to do for you and the children."

Ethel looked confused. "Huh? W-what could that be? You giving us a place to stay for a while is more than enough."

"Eugene and I don't want the kids to go into foster care, or back to your relatives."

There was a glazed look in Ethel's eyes. The tone of her voice was raspy, as if she'd suddenly developed a mild case of laryngitis. "You mean in case I was to die while we living with y'all?"

"Well, that's not what I meant. There are other reasons why you may have to give up the kids. Say you became disabled, or decide to move into a retirement home."

"All of that done crossed my mind before," she admitted. "I force myself not to think about it too much though. But I don't want you to think we plan on staying here forever. I don't want them kids to think I can't take care of them."

"Ethel, let's look at the big picture. Even if you find a new place you like and can afford, you still may have to go into a facility eventually. The kids wouldn't be able to fend for themselves."

"If I'm lucky, they'll be grown by then."

"Cynthia might be. But the boys are only eleven and twelve. We're talking about several more years. Do you honestly think you can keep working and looking after them that long?"

"I could with God's help. He ain't never let me down yet."

"Well, this time He's working on your behalf through Eugene and me."

"I already figured that out. It wasn't no coincidence that you had to have that operation and would need help. Plus y'all was able to hunt me down after all these years."

"Ethel . . ." I paused and walked over and took her hands in mine. "I'm going to cut to the chase. Eugene and I want to adopt the children."

CHAPTER 22

Ethel's reaction to my statement surprised me. Her eyes got big and her mouth dropped open. She snatched her hands out of mine so fast, it made my head spin. "S-say what? Y'all want to *adopt* my babies?"

"Yes."

"Good gracious alive. I couldn't burden y'all like that. It's already enough of a burden with us moving in."

"It would *not* be a 'burden.' It would be a blessing. Eugene and I have wanted children for years. For us this would be a dream come true. And you can rest assured that your great-grandchildren will be well taken care of. With adoption we'd have all the legal issues covered."

The stunned expression on Ethel's face worried me. She cleared her throat, bowed her head, and stared at the floor. "Leaving them with good people like you and Eugene would be a dream come true for me and the kids too. Even if my niece took them in, she wouldn't be able to give them the wonderful life you and Eugene can provide."

"If you want to take some time to think about this, that's fine. Maybe a few weeks? Or a month?"

After a few moments she looked up with tears in her eyes. But there was also a smile on her face. "If I took a few weeks or a month to think more about it, I'd still come up with the same answer, so I ain't going to waste no time. Let's get them kids adopted. I'd hate to put it off and . . . well, ain't nobody promised tomorrow."

"I know," I mumbled. "I just don't want you to feel pressured. But I appreciate your not wanting to put it off."

Ethel looked very relieved; I was sorry I hadn't brought up adoption before now. "The sooner I make some real arrangements for myself and the kids, the better I'll feel. At least I won't go to bed every night now wondering what's going to happen to them after I'm gone. They ain't perfect, so you and Eugene will have the same ups and downs other parents have. But they ain't bad eggs neither. Except . . . well, Cynthia will need some extra attention, and maybe some professional help like I already mentioned to you."

"And like I've already mentioned to you, we'll get her all the help she needs. But first things first. We'll deal with Cynthia later. I still think we should get you and the boys moved by the next week or so. Is that all right with you?"

"I . . . guess."

"Hopefully, by Christmas, you'll all be settled in and we can enjoy the holiday."

"I just thought of something else," Ethel said, giving me a skeptical look.

My heart immediately began to race. I silently prayed that after all we'd just discussed and agreed to, she wasn't having second thoughts.

"What is it?" I asked with hesitation.

"I just paid the rent for December yesterday. I doubt very seriously if the new owner would refund part of my money if we move out next week. It wouldn't seem fair to me for him to keep my money and I ain't even sleeping there no more. On top of that, I got a feeling he ain't going to give me my security deposit back. The first time he came into the apartment when he was inspecting it to see if he wanted to buy the building, he made a few comments about how the boys had left holes in the wall from tacking up posters and whatnot. Then he made a big stink about some hair dye Cynthia had spilled on the hallway carpet and how much it was going to cost him to 'restore' everything."

"Don't worry about your security deposit. You won't need it. You won't have any financial problems as long as you live with us. But it's a good thing you've paid your rent for this month. Even if you and the boys move in with us next week, you might have to leave some of the heavy things behind until Eugene can get somebody to haul it away. However, if you move out next week, the new owner would probably love the fact that you're gone. That way he'd be able to paint and do whatever else he needs to do. Then his daughter could move in sooner."

Ethel gave me a brief, thoughtful look and quickly went on speaking. "I know your extra bedrooms is already fully furnished, so ain't no need for me to bring none of that broke-down stuff we been using for so many years. I got a few furniture items I'd like to keep though. But I'd hate to clutter up your garage."

"If you don't want to store anything in our garage, we can still put it in a storage facility for as long as you need."

Ethel laughed quietly. "You got a solution for everything, ain't you?"

"Not everything," I said with a shrug.

After we had eaten our lunch, Ethel insisted on doing the laundry. While she was in the utility room, I decided to check in with Min-jee and Genelle.

"Genelle is with a vendor and I can't talk long. Your buddy Mr. Yamaguchi is here. His feet have almost finished soaking and I'll need to take care of him in a few minutes," Min-jee said, unable to stifle a laugh. "I know he came in last month and you spent a lot of time working on him. But today his toenails

look like Fritos." Min-jee let out a loud laugh. I tried
not to, but after a few seconds of holding it in, I guffawed like a hyena.

"You'd better be nice to him," I advised. "Not only
is he our most lovable longtime client, he's also one of
our biggest tippers," I reminded her. Then I laughed
again. "Okay, on a more serious note, I need to up-
date you and G on a couple of things."

"Like what?"

"We're going to move Ethel and her family in with
us. Within the next week or so, I hope. And, God
willing, we're going to get the adoption process going
as soon as possible."

"Genelle told me about your wanting to adopt. I
was shocked, to say the least. Are you absolutely sure
this is what you want to do? What about Eugene?"

"He wants to do it as much as I do. You should see
how giddy he is with those boys. He'd love to adopt
them. Ethel was a little reluctant about it when I first
mentioned it to her."

"Oh? Well, that's not a good sign. What if you and
Eugene get the paperwork started and she changes
her mind?"

"I don't think that's going to happen."

"Then why was she being reluctant?"

"She's been having issues with Cynthia. Even knowing that the new owner wants his daughter to move
into their unit, Cynthia is refusing to leave the neighborhood."

"It doesn't sound like she's going to have a choice!"

"I know. She's real close with one of their neighbors and has practically moved in with them."

"Until when?"

"I don't know."

"So, tell me, what is Ethel going to do about her? She's still a minor and the law says she can't do what she wants yet."

"Don't mention the law. Ethel is scared to death that if she calls the authorities, child protective services will get involved and put her great-granddaughter in foster care. Poor Ethel. She's losing so much sleep at night! When she got here this morning, she looked like she'd been mauled."

"Kids can wear you down to a frazzle. If Bob and I didn't stay on our toes and run such a tight ship at all times, there is no telling what our situation would be like. Thank God, ours are easier to manage than most kids. If Cynthia's acting a fool, I'm pretty sure that the folks she moved in with won't put up with it long. They might be the ones to call the authorities."

"I've thought about that. But I'm sure it won't come to that."

Eugene and I filed a petition to adopt the children the very next day.

CHAPTER 23

It had been ten days since we'd filed the adoption papers. The social worker handling our case assured us that after our background checks had been completed, and if we met the necessary requirements, the adoptions would be finalized within six months. "Typically, it takes from three months to a year. But since the birth parents are not in the picture, it may even take less time in your case," she told us.

Ethel had signed over her rights as their guardian, and we assured her that it would not end or minimize her authority in her great-grandchildren's lives. But I was still a little apprehensive that something might happen to derail everything.

What if she changed her mind after discussing the situation with her relatives? She could pack up and head to Bugtussle, Kentucky, and we'd never see them again. What if one of her cash-strapped relatives in South Central or Bugtussle wanted the kids so they could collect the Social Security benefits, and hired a slick lawyer and took us to court? The adoption could be put on hold for months, maybe even years. And then it might not be processed in our favor at all.

I couldn't figure out why I was having such outlandish and pessimistic thoughts. First of all, Ethel was not the type to go back on her word. Besides, she'd seemed really relieved when I'd first told her we wanted to adopt the kids.

Eugene wasn't worried about a thing, and I didn't let him know how worried I was. He would have dismissed my concerns and that would have made me feel even worse. But I knew I'd be on pins and needles until everything was over. I was becoming a nervous wreck. I prayed that all this new excitement didn't have any more negative impacts on my health.

It had been four weeks since I'd had my surgery. Dr. Miller was pleased with how well I was doing. He was grinning from ear to ear by the time my checkup ended today. "I'm pleased to see that there is no more swelling, you don't look as tired as you did the last time I saw you, and you've lost eight pounds." He grinned as he peered at me over the top of his horn-rimmed glasses. "How are things going with you otherwise?"

A smile formed on my face that reached from one side to the other.

"That broad smile must mean things are going well, right?"

"Better than well. My husband and I have decided

to adopt. I am nervous about it though. But just a little. I haven't mentioned it to Eugene because I don't want him to feel the same way."

Dr. Miller's eyebrows shot up. "That's wonderful news and nothing to be nervous about. I'm delighted to know that you didn't waste any time. Typically, adoption procedures can drag on for years. My nephew and his wife filled out an application to adopt two years ago and they're still waiting."

"I know it could take a while. That's why we decided not to put it off." I didn't want to mention all of the details about when and whose children we were adopting—in case things fell through. Genelle's and Min-jee's reactions were enough for now.

"Being a parent is such an honor. My wife and I had always wanted a large family, but we were only blessed with three—a boy and two girls. However, we have eight grandchildren now, and another one on the way."

"I am so happy for you," I said. "I'm sure they've enriched your life tremendously."

"Most definitely." Dr. Miller's demeanor changed so abruptly, it scared me. He blinked and rubbed the side of his head. "Frankly, raising children can be hectic and challenging at times. But I'm sure you are well aware of that. However, at the end of the day, it's one of the most important and rewarding roles in a person's life." Dr. Miller gave me a somber look as he continued. "I hope that things work out for you and that you'll be blessed with many healthy children." He scratched the side of his head, then grinned again. "Congratulations to you and your husband. Have a merry Christmas."

Eugene usually played golf with one of the partners at his law firm on the weekends. He'd left the house with his golf clubs at ten a.m. on Saturday, right after we'd devoured the scrumptious Denver omelets I'd prepared. I had a busy day planned myself. I had offered to help Ethel finish packing everything she wanted to bring to the house.

After I cleaned up the kitchen, I took a shower, covered my hair with a scarf, and put on a T-shirt and the most comfortable jeans I owned. Then I headed to Ethel's apartment. By the time I got there, she and the boys had already boxed up most of their clothing and other personal items, so I didn't expect to be at her place too long.

About an hour into the packing, Ethel started wheezing and swaying from side to side. We were in her bedroom, going through linen and bedroom items she'd been hoarding that she no longer wanted.

"You get some rest and let me and the boys finish up," I insisted. I didn't give her time to protest. I took her by the arm and led her to the living-room couch.

I had forgotten to take my meds the day before, so

I was feeling pretty light-headed too. I promised myself that I'd go to bed early tonight. A couple extra
hours' sleep usually restored my equilibrium, so I wasn't
too much concerned about my health. But Ethel was.

"Rosemary, you don't look too good yourself. It
looks like half the blood done drained out of your face.
Why don't you sit down too?" she said as she plopped
down on the couch, patting the spot next to her.

"Pfffttt," I responded with a wave of my hand. "I
feel okay. Sometimes I get a little dizzy when I move
around too fast. I'd rather keep working so we can
get this done and be on our way." I didn't wait to
hear her response. I rushed back out of the room.

While the boys were in their room, I decided to do
what I could in the kitchen. Several neighbors had
come over and taken dishes, cookware, and everything else they wanted that Ethel didn't want to hang
on to.

While I was wiping off the kitchen counter, I heard
the back door creak open. When I turned around, I
was surprised to see it cracked open just wide enough
for me to see one side of Cynthia's face.

"Hi, Miss Rosemary. You in here by yourself?" she
asked in a low tone.

"Yes, I am. And you don't have to call me 'Miss'
Rosemary. Just Rosemary is fine. And Eugene is just
Eugene."

"Okay, Rosemary," she mumbled. "I . . . um . . . I heard you was over here helping pack up."

"Yes, and we're almost finished. Don't you think you should check to see if there's anything here that you'd like to keep?"

She shook her head. "I already got all of my good stuff." She looked over my shoulder toward the door that led to the living room. "Where is everybody?"

"The boys are in their room packing. Ethel is resting in the living room. She's probably asleep, but I can wake her. I'm sure she'd be happy to see you."

Cynthia quickly held up her hand and shook her head. "Oh, I don't want to wake her up! I just wanted to make sure she's doing all right. I heard she's been feeling weak and stuff."

I waved my hand dismissively. "Oh, it's nothing to worry about. She's just a little under the weather. And packing and moving is tiresome."

"Yeah. Um . . . I was hoping I'd catch you by yourself. I wanted to thank you for all the things you and Mr. Eugene are doing for my family. I know Granny's mad at me, so I am not ready to talk to her again yet. The same with the boys." Cynthia looked over my shoulder again.

"I am sure that when you're ready to talk to them, they'll be happy."

"I guess Granny told you a lot about me."

"I know you've had some problems. But for every problem there is a solution."

"I just got tired of being told what to do all the time. I have to come straight home from school to look after the boys and get dinner started. I have to clean the house. I don't have time to spend with my friends. And I don't have time just to be a teenager. All the kids I know get to hang out on weekends and have fun. Me, I'm in the house mopping floors, dusting, doing laundry, and washing dishes. When I go to school, I'm so wound up, I get mad and jealous of the other kids because they're having all the fun."

I sniffed and gave Cynthia the most sympathetic look I could manage. "I know just what you mean. I went through the same things when I was your age."

"Did you run away from home too?"

"Oh no! I knew that would only make matters worse!" I exclaimed with so much vigor, spit flew out both sides of my mouth. I paused and said in a gentler tone, "That never entered my mind. I knew that I was much better off at home with my parents than I would have been in the streets. But I still only wanted to hang out and have a good time with my cool friends. My parents telling me what to do, and what not to do, got on my nerves. But I'm glad they did. It didn't take long for me to realize that I could do what my parents told me to do, and still hang out with my friends and have fun. All I had to do was organize my time better, prioritize my responsibilities, and make the right decisions about everything I did. Otherwise, I probably would have ended up in a situation I wouldn't have liked."

"Like my mama and her mama? Dead?"

"Well, that's pretty extreme, but I could have ended up like them," I admitted.

Cynthia stared at me for a few moments and glanced at the door again. "I better go before they come in here and get in my face."

I held up my hand. "Don't go yet. Wait another minute or so. I'm glad you came. It was nice to see you again. I hope everything is going the way you thought it would for you."

The expression on Cynthia's face changed dramatically. The way her eyes widened and her lips quivered, she looked like she was going to scream. "Are you kidding? It's already turning into a big old mess. Ciara's mama is almost as bad as Granny. I have to help clean the house and follow her rules too. How do grown folks expect teenagers to be happy if they keep controlling us and putting their noses in our business?"

"I used to wonder about that myself. But they're just doing their job as parents. We don't know anything when we are first born. And even after we've been around fourteen or fifteen years and think we know everything, we don't know the half of it. We haven't had time to figure things out. That's why it's so important for parents, or guardians in some cases, to guide their children, as well as to provide for them, and nurture and protect them. Don't you think so?"

"Yeah," she muttered.

"Ethel told me that you're on the honor roll."

"I am. Two years straight now. Why?"

"Then you're a very smart girl."

She hunched her shoulders. "I guess so."

"Can I show you something?"

"I guess so," Cynthia said again with a perplexed look on her face this time. "What?"

I turned on the faucet, picked up one of the glasses I had dried and set on the counter, and filled it with water. "You see the water in this glass?"

"So?"

I poured the water into the sink.

"What did you do that for?"

"Now watch this." I filled the glass again and poured the water into another glass. "When I dumped the water into the sink, it went all over the place because it had no boundaries. It did what it wanted and now it's gone down the drain, never to be seen again. When I transferred it to another glass, there were boundaries. The water will stay contained until I dispose of it or drink it. Imagine the things I could do with it in the glass. I could make tea, lemonade, or even one of my old-school favorites, Kool-Aid."

" 'Kool-Aid'?" Cynthia guffawed. "The only black folks I know that still drink that are the ones in the hood. Granny don't even buy it."

"I grew up on it, and I still buy it every now and then. What I'm trying to show you is that the water would serve a much better purpose in the glass than if I poured it into the sink."

Cynthia blinked. "So what? You might pour it into the sink anyway. What does a glass-of-water demonstration have to do with anything?"

"If you think of it in terms of life in general, it has a lot to do with everything. Without boundaries and structure, anything could happen. Unfortunately, when there are no boundaries, or when they are ignored, bad things are more likely to happen."

Cynthia blinked again and bit her bottom lip. "I think I know what you mean." Then she nodded and said slowly, "Um, I heard the boys and Granny will have their own rooms in your house."

"That's right. When we start our Christmas shopping next week, I'll let them pick out what they want for their rooms so they can make them more personal."

Cynthia gave me a sorrowful look. "Christmas," she said, blinking back a tear. "This will be the first Christmas . . ." She sucked in a deep breath and stopped talking. After she cleared her throat, she went on. "I wish . . ." She paused again and blinked some more.

I had never seen such a profoundly sad look on a person's face until now.

"I wish my mama had lived long enough to see how nice some people really are." She took a deep breath and asked, "Will you still do my nails someday?"

"Absolutely. As often as you want."

"Oh, okay." Cynthia squinted and said shyly, "Ciara's mama told me that you and Mr. Eugene filled out some adoption papers. She said Granny told her it was so she won't have to keep worrying about what would happen to us if something happens to her. Is that true?" Before I could answer, she asked, "I mean, does the adoption include me, even though I'm living with Ciara's family?"

"Yes, we did file adoption papers, and, yes, we included you."

"I didn't know a person could adopt somebody without them knowing about it, or agreeing to it."

"Yes, they can. You're still a minor. Ethel is still your legal guardian, no matter where you live. When the adoptions are finalized, you and your brothers will be part of our family."

There was a glazed look in her eyes now. It was hard to believe how many different expressions I'd seen on her face in just a few moments. And then she gave me a tight smile.

"Is that all right with you?" I asked softly.

She nodded. "I just didn't know if you and Mr. Eugene would have room for somebody like me."

"Cynthia, we will always have room for you, no matter what."

"Okay." She smiled again, wider this time. "Well, I'll let you get back to whatever you were doing. Thanks for showing me that glass trick. I'll remember it in case I have to use it on one of my kids someday."

CHAPTER 24

I didn't mention Cynthia's visit and our conversation in the kitchen to anyone. I felt so sorry for that poor child. Even though Eugene and I had been foster parents to two teenagers, my experience with this age group was somewhat limited. However, I could tell that Cynthia was not a "bad" girl, per se. She was confused, and maybe a little delusional. In the meantime she hadn't cut herself off from her family completely and I was glad that she was comfortable expressing herself to me. But I was as worried about her as Ethel.

We transported as much of her property to my house in my car as we could fit. Eugene had made arrangements for movers to pick up everything else that she wanted to keep in our garage, and to haul the rest to Goodwill and the Salvation Army next weekend. Ethel and the boys went home with me that evening.

* * *

Later that night, with Ethel standing next to us, Eugene and I asked Eddie and Anthony to sit down on the living-room couch so we could talk to them. "Boys, we need to go over a few things with you," I stated.

Eddie gulped and whirled around to look at his brother. Then he looked back up at us. "I hope y'all didn't change your mind about adopting us!" he wailed.

"Or letting us live here," Anthony whimpered with a frightened look on his face.

"Not at all," Eugene assured them, standing with his arms folded across his chest. "We just wanted to let you know how happy we are to have you in our family." He paused and looked at Ethel. "All of you."

"And look-a-here, you two," Ethel said in a loud, stern tone as she wagged her finger at the boys. "Y'all better continue to behave as good as you done with me. That includes doing the same chores here that you did in our apartment, and any new ones that go with this house. And everything will have to be done before you watch TV, hang out with your friends, or fiddle around on that nice computer in Eugene's office."

"Can we invite some of our friends from the old neighborhood over every now and then?" Anthony wanted to know.

"And can we visit them?" Eddie asked.

"You can still do all of that and more. We encourage you to make new friends at your new school and become acquainted with the kids in this neighborhood."

"And don't even think about bringing no drugs into this nice Christian house!" Ethel added, shaking her finger in the boys' direction again.

"Drugs?" the boys shrieked at the same time.

"I don't even know what drugs look like," Eddie said sharply, giving us a hopeless look.

"We would never do something that stupid. Honest to God, we won't," Anthony vowed. "Drugs are for idiots," he added.

"Ethel, I'm sure we won't have to worry about that," I said as I gently stroked her arm.

"Praise God. Hallelujah." She waved her hands in the air and danced a jig for a few seconds. Eddie and Anthony looked embarrassed, but they laughed along with us.

It was hard to believe that just a few hours earlier, Ethel had been so sluggish. An hour later, she started cleaning areas in the house that didn't need it, and she insisted on cooking dinner so Eugene and I could spend what was left of the evening resting.

On Sunday afternoon Min-jee brought Jared and Michael, her sons aged ten and twelve, respectively, to the house to meet my new family. Her husband, Bob, was a pilot for a major airline. He had been contacted at the last minute to cover for a sick colleague, who had been scheduled to fly to Salt Lake City. Genelle showed up an hour later with her three teenagers: two boys and a girl. Her husband, Patrick, who was the principal at the new school the boys would be attending, had come too. The boys were all close in age, so they hit it off right away. Genelle's eldest, her seventeen-year-old daughter, Helene, was not the least bit interested in going fishing with Eugene, Patrick, and the boys, nor was she interested in sitting around with three middle-aged wives and an elderly lady. She promptly whipped out her smartphone and called up her boyfriend. The minute he entered the house, the two of them bolted.

"Ro, it looks like things are working out just the way you wanted," Min-jee said with a twinkle in her eyes I hadn't seen since she'd given birth to her last child.

She, Genelle, and I were sitting at my kitchen table drinking English tea. Ethel was in her room watching a talk show with Brother O as one of the guests. It was playing on the flat-screen TV we'd purchased for her room.

"Well, almost. Ethel is reluctant to talk about her great-granddaughter not being here, but I know she wants to," I replied.

"Is Cynthia still living with the neighbors?" Genelle asked.

"As far as we know," I replied.

"Honey, let me give you some advice. Don't get too comfortable just yet," Genelle asserted.

"I'd like to know what that's supposed to mean?" I snapped, rolling my neck and giving her the most exasperated look I could manage.

"I'd like to know too," Min-jee piped in.

"Not too many people would do what you and Eugene are doing. Not even for blood relatives," Genelle stated. "I don't think your purpose on earth is to be anybody's savior."

I gave her a puzzled look. From the corner of my eye, I could see Min-jee looked just as puzzled.

"Taking in a distressed family? That's not being a 'savior.' That's being generous and caring," Min-jee said. "Is that what you think about my parents adopting me?"

Genelle held up both of her hands. "Now don't take things out of context. Your situation was a whole lot different. You were an abandoned child. But Ethel has family and other sources she could have gone to for help."

I narrowed my eyes and glared at Genelle. It must have made her uneasy because she immediately began to fidget in her chair.

"Let me ask you this. If something were to happen to you and Patrick, wouldn't you want the *best* for your kids?"

"I would, and so would my family. I have relatives

all over the country, and a bunch in Jamaica, where my grandparents were born," Genelle said defensively. "They'd step in and do whatever they needed to do."

"Yes, 'needed to do' is one thing. But how many people do you think would *want* to take in four additional family members, especially ones not related to them by blood?" I shot back.

"You and Eugene are the only ones I know," she mumbled.

"Yes, because we *wanted* to. Not because we're trying to be martyrs or saviors, or whatever you want to call us. The bottom line is, Ethel and those children needed help and we gave it to them. And just as important, Eugene and I wanted a family. I hope I don't have to keep repeating that for the rest of my life!" I was getting exasperated and I refused to hide it.

"Calm down, Ro. I'm on your side. If what you've done makes you happy, I'm happy for you," Genelle admitted. "If you ever need any help adjusting to your new situation, just let me know."

"The same goes for me," Min-jee tossed in.

When Eugene, Patrick, and the boys returned with ten medium-size bass, they went out to the back porch to clean them. Genelle and Min-jee helped Ethel and me add more tinsel and ornaments to the gigantic Christmas tree Eugene had put up in the living room last week.

My family and I spent the next few days getting

ready for Christmas. We visited several malls to purchase more gifts. We attended one of Brother O's performances at his church, which was so amazing *and* G-rated that Ethel and I immediately became two of his biggest fans. When we got home, we watched a movie on DVD that Eugene and I had loved for years, *Miracle on 34th Street*. Ethel and the kids had never seen it and they loved it too.

"It's going to take me a while to get used to living such a laid-back life," Ethel commented as we were about to turn in for the night. "This time last year on the same day, I was working my fingers to the bone, serving drinks to Mrs. Goldstein's company. I was so worn-out when she let me off that night, I fell asleep on the bus on my way home and missed my stop."

"Well, you'll never have to ride another bus if you don't want to," I assured her.

"Good night, Rosemary. I'll see you in the morning." Ethel turned to leave, and then she turned back around. "Oh, Rosemary, one more thing. Thank you again."

"Thank you." I smiled.

The next morning, which was Christmas Eve day, we attended a morning program at Ethel's church in South Central. That's where we met some of her other family members, including the niece who had offered to be responsible for the children. Vernell Perkins was just as warm and friendly as Ethel. During a break in the service, she took me aside and told me, "When I heard y'all was going to take over with the kids, I cried like a baby and thanked God from the bottom of my heart. I would have took them in if I had to, but I'm glad they ended up in a much better place. I just hope Cynthia come to her senses and get her tail over to y'all too."

"I'm sure she will when she's ready," I replied.

Later in the evening, we attended a program at the church we belonged to. We hadn't attended service since before my surgery, so it was nice to be among the friendly congregation again. As we were leaving, Reverend Updike shook hands with Eugene and hugged us all.

"Rosemary, it's good to see you looking so healthy, praise the Lord. And I'm as pleased as I can be about you and Eugene's decision to adopt." He paused and looked at Ethel, then at the boys. "And what a fine-looking family! I hope all of y'all will be very happy from now on."

"We will be," Eugene said with a firm nod.

Everybody was in a giddy mood when we got home. After dinner, Anthony wrapped the outside of our front door with red-and-green-striped Christmas paper. He taped a huge silver bow in the center so that it looked like a gigantic Christmas present. Eddie, our future baker, had impressed us all when he made five dozen sugar cookies from scratch. When we couldn't eat any more, we stuffed what was left into ziplock bags; then the boys and I drove to a seedy area and passed them out to homeless people.

"I hope we can do this every year from now on," Eddie said on our way home. "I like doing nice things for people."

"We will do it every year. I like doing nice things for people too," I said.

CHAPTER 25

Ethel had given up her job at the convenience store in her old neighborhood, but she still kept in touch with some of her former neighbors. The only household she was reluctant to telephone belonged to the Weatherspoons, the home where Cynthia had moved. Ethel had called over there five or six times since she'd moved in with us. Each time she'd called, she'd been told that Cynthia had "just left." Ethel finally gave up.

I didn't tell her that when I called to see how Cynthia was getting along, she was always available and quite eager to speak with me.

"Tell Granny I'm sorry I keep missing her calls. But let her know I'm thinking about her and the boys, and she doesn't need to worry about me," she said the last time I spoke to her, four days prior.

I didn't like keeping things from Ethel, but my gut told me that unless Cynthia came around on her own, this cycle would continue.

When I got up at eight o'clock on Christmas morning, I immediately called the Weatherspoons' residence to wish Cynthia a merry Christmas, and to let her know that there were several gifts for her under our tree. I was stunned when Ciara told me, "She don't live here no more. She moved out last night and we don't know where she went."

I was crushed. Ethel had been in good spirits for the past few days, and I didn't want to bring her down by sharing this news with her. I decided to wait and tell her after Christmas. But I told Eugene right away. He was in our master bathroom shaving his head.

"And you haven't told Ethel?" he asked, dropping his razor into the sink and gazing at me with his eyes squinted. He looked comical standing there with one side of his head covered in shaving cream.

"Not yet. I think we should wait until tomorrow. I'd hate to ruin the holiday for her," I replied.

"Well, I have a feeling the holiday, and every other day, was ruined for her the first time Cynthia ran away."

"You're probably right. But I still think we shouldn't tell her right now. Maybe by the time Ethel calls over there again, she'll be back."

Ethel was still in a good mood when we all gathered in the living room to open our presents. The boys were happy with the new clothes and a slew of popular video games and other boy toys we had bought them. But they were ecstatic when they saw their new iPhones and laptops. In addition to an eighteen-piece set of cookware for me and a fishing rod for Eugene, Ethel had knitted us each a red sweater. Eugene had given her a new bathrobe and I'd given her a five-hundred dollar gift certificate.

One of the few material items that Ethel had ever mentioned to me that she'd always wanted a Gucci purse, like the one her former employer owned, which she had purchased on Rodeo Drive. I gave her the same purse. When she saw it, she was so overwhelmed and jubilant, she laughed until she cried. After kissing the purse, she gently placed it on the coffee table and admired it, laughing and clapping her hands like a seal.

"Rosemary, Eugene, y'all done made me so happy! I don't care if I die tomorrow," she sniffled.

"Well, don't do that anytime soon. We love having you and want you to stick around for a very long time," Eugene said with his voice faltering. In all the years I'd known him, I hadn't seen him look this emotional since his parents passed. He turned his head, but I still saw a few tears trickle down the side of his face.

"Cynthia told me one time that when she grew up and got a good job, she was going to buy me this same purse. She's going to be tickled to death when I tell her I got one now!" Ethel squealed. She was over the moon, until she picked up the landline in the kitchen and called the Weatherspoons' house a few minutes later.

I braced myself, knowing what was coming.

Right after she asked to speak to Cynthia, her face dropped. She abruptly hung up and looked at me. There were more tears in her eyes, and her voice was just above a whisper when she spoke. "That girl took off from there last night, and Ciara claims she don't know where she went. I'm so tired of worrying about that child," she said, choking on a sob. "I just hope she don't get herself into a pickle she can't get out of." Ethel heaved out a loud, heavy sigh and shook her head. "Where could she be?"

"Ethel, she's going to be just fine. I'm sure of that," I said tentatively. "Does she have a Snapchat account? If so, we'll check it. That's where some kids like to post every move they make."

"Snap*what*?"

"Social media." I sighed. From the confused look on Ethel's face, I realized she had no idea what I was talking about, so I didn't go any further on that subject. "Why don't you go in the living room with Eugene and the boys, and I'll finish the cooking. Or go to your room and watch a few Christmas movies on the Hallmark Channel, all right? That'll keep you occupied."

"I'd rather stay in this kitchen and help you cook," Ethel insisted as she began mixing the dressing I had already started.

Around three p.m., Eugene and I called up some of our relatives. We were very happy to hear that Lawrence's mother-in-law was doing so much better. Ethel called up some of her relatives and friends, but her calls were all very brief. I had a feeling she'd cut them short because Cynthia's name had come up.

Eugene and I exchanged gifts with several of our neighbors each year. Most of them had already come and gone.

We finally sat down to eat dinner at four p.m. Before we could proceed, someone knocked on our front door. Eugene answered it. Another neighbor had come to drop off gifts and pick up theirs.

"Hopefully, we'll get through dinner without any more interruptions," Eugene commented.

He was seated at the head of the table, looking totally ridiculous with a Santa Claus hat on his shiny head. He cleared his throat and slowly glanced around the table. The smile on his face and the look in his eyes were so touching—I had to force myself not to cry.

"Ethel, Eddie, and Anthony, Ro and I would like to let you all know that you're the best Christmas gift we've ever received. We had almost lost all hope of ever becoming parents. I hope you are all as happy as we are."

"When can we start calling you Daddy and Rosemary Mama?" Eddie asked.

"Why not start today?" I said, getting it out quickly before I started crying.

"What do we call Granny now, since we got a new mama and daddy?" Anthony wanted to know.

"Y'all better still call me Granny," Ethel advised. "Because that's what I'll always be."

We all laughed.

Before anyone could speak again, someone else knocked on the front door.

"I'll get it. That's got to be the Fongs or the Lombardos from across the street. They're the only ones who haven't come by yet." I wiped my hands on my napkin and trotted to the living room. I didn't bother to look out the peephole. When I flung open the door, I did a double take. Cynthia stood in front of me with a puppy-dog expression on her face. There was a taxicab in front of the house, and its motor was still running. "W-what are you doing here?" I asked in a raspy tone. "Where have you been?"

"I . . . I slept in the Greyhound bus station last night," she muttered with her cloudy, red-rimmed eyes darting from side to side.

"Why didn't you come here?" I asked.

"I was too scared."

"Cynthia, there is no reason for you to be scared. We were all worried sick about you."

She sniffed, rubbed her nose, and told me, "I know, and I'm sorry. Anyway, I thought about that glass of water a lot," she mumbled.

"What?"

"Is it too late for me?"

"What do you mean?" I glanced at the cab and then back at her. The look in her eyes was so distraught, I had to blink hard to hold back my tears. I forced myself to smile. "Do you want to see your granny? We're just about to have dinner. I'm sure everyone would be pleased if you'd join us."

"My stuff is in the cab. If I can't stay here too, I'll go on about my business."

I was so flabbergasted that I could barely form words again. "You want to move in with us?"

She nodded. "If it's not too late."

"No, it's not too late! It's never too late! Come on in," I said with my heart beating about a mile a minute.

"Let me pay the taxi and get my stuff."

"I'll help you—"

"That's all right. I don't have much."

I stood in the doorway and waited for Cynthia to return. The lump in my throat was so huge, my throat ached when I swallowed.

When she lurched over the threshold, I grabbed her backpack and shabby suitcase and set them on the floor by the coatrack.

"You can unpack after you eat."

"Will I have my own room too?"

"Yes, you will."

I put my arm around her shoulder and steered her

to the dining room. As soon as we appeared in the doorway, every jaw at the table dropped. Words could not describe the look on Ethel's face.

"I'm sorry, Granny," Cynthia said. "Please don't be mad at me."

While Ethel was wobbling up from her chair, Cynthia ran into her arms. They embraced and sobbed for a few minutes, and then Cynthia sat down next to Ethel. She stopped crying and looked around the table. "I wanted to come over here before now." She looked directly at Eugene and then at me. "I didn't know if you nice normal people wanted me."

"We do want you," Eugene said. "You're part of our family now, sweetie."

"You ought to see how many gifts there are under the tree for you," Anthony blurted out.

"Huh?" Cynthia gasped and looked from me to Eugene. "I didn't expect any gifts," she said. "I . . . I don't care what they are, I really appreciate getting them."

"Rosemary and I got the best gift of all," Eugene said. "The gift of family."

"Amen," I said, lifting my hands above my head and waving them. I had never felt so joyous in my life. And it couldn't have happened at a better time of the year.

Ethel sniffled as she dabbed Cynthia's dried chapped lips with her napkin. "Baby, you look so dehydrated," she said. Then she looked at Eddie. "Boy, go get your sister a glass of water."

"A glass of water? What's that supposed to do?" Eddie snickered.

Cynthia looked at me with a knowing smile and winked. "It could do a whole lot for me," she said, looking around the table again. "Merry Christmas, everybody."

"Merry Christmas," the rest of us chorused.

And with that, our family was complete.

EPILOGUE

Six months later

The adoptions were finalized earlier this month. My life had become so hectic since last year, I could barely keep up. We were busier than ever at the salon. I had PTA, parent/teacher meetings, and soccer games to attend on a regular basis. And I spent twice as much time shopping as before. Our children were growing out of their clothes so fast, we had to buy new ones every other month.

All three were doing better than Eugene and I had expected. But the one that really surprised us was Cynthia. After only eight sessions with the therapist I'd taken her to, it seemed like she had developed a whole new personality. She was one of the most pleasant teenagers I'd ever encountered. It was hard to believe she was the same girl who had run away from home, talked back to Ethel, bickered with her brothers when they teased her, and walked around with a scowl on her face. However, she had to be occasionally "encouraged" to stay on top of her household responsibilities and choose clothing more appropriate for a girl her age when I took her shopping.

Cynthia had made a lot of new friends, and she kept in touch with all of her old friends. She'd even developed her first crush on a boy in our neighborhood. Every time she mentioned him, she glowed. "Oh, Mama!" (Every time one of my children called me Mama, *I* glowed.) "David is going to be a lawyer like Daddy. You think I should marry him when we finish college?" she asked me last week.

"Let's discuss this more when you finish college," I replied with a laugh.

Eugene enjoyed taking the boys fishing so much, he purchased his own boat last month. They went to Malibu Pier almost every Saturday now.

Ethel and the kids joined our church, and they paid regular visits to their extended family in South Central. Eugene and I had accompanied them a few times.

Earlier this month my sister-in-law's mother recovered fully from her stroke. Instead of waiting to visit our relatives in Connecticut for Christmas this year, we went a week after Lena's mother had come home from the hospital. All of the kids hit it off right away.

Ethel gushed and beamed during the whole visit. "Rosemary, you and Eugene done made me so happy, I told y'all once before that I don't care if I die tomorrow. I still feel the same way. And when I do go home to live with the Lord, I don't want nobody to mourn my death. I'll be in a much better place and I done had a good life, so I want my passing to be celebrated. If at all possible, please get that gospel rapper Brother O—we all love him so much—to sing at my funeral."

Ethel didn't die "tomorrow." We had a few more weeks of amazing time with her.

But one morning last week, she had a massive heart attack and died two hours later. Eugene and I, and all three of our children, were with her when she took her last breath at the hospital.

We covered the travel expenses for some of Ethel's relatives in Bugtussle, Kentucky, to come to California and say good-bye to her. (That is, the ones who were not too superstitious to fly.)

Brother O canceled another engagement without hesitation so he'd be available to perform at her funeral, or "celebration," I should say.

Ethel would have been proud.

DISCUSSION QUESTIONS

1. Do you think Rosemary and Eugene got close to Ethel and her great-grandchildren too soon?

2. Rosemary and Eugene were so desperate to be parents, they were willing to adopt older children and ones with special needs. With their hectic lifestyle and the challenges that come with hard-to-place children, would this have been a good decision or a bad one?

3. Ethel Perkins was a proud and independent woman who worked hard to take care of her great-grandchildren on her own. But it didn't take long for her to decide to let Rosemary and Eugene adopt them. She felt that at her age, making plans for their future was something she could not put off. What do you think about her quick decision?

4. Min-jee and Genelle were concerned about Rosemary getting involved in Ethel's problems after only knowing her for less than a month. If you had a friend in a similar situation, would you intervene or keep your opinions to yourself?

5. Do you think Eugene and Rosemary's marriage was so strong, they'd stay together even if they never had children?

6. Because of Eugene's and Rosemary's jobs, they interacted with a lot of celebrities and other affluent people. But they were humble and very down-to-earth. If you interacted with celebrities on a regular basis, how would you keep yourself grounded?

7. Ethel's hard work and guidance hadn't kept her daughter and granddaughter from associating with the wrong people and paying for it with their lives. Before Eugene and Rosemary entered her life, Ethel worked two jobs so she could afford to move. Was she unrealistic to think that by raising the children in a better environment, they'd be less likely to end up like her daughter and granddaughter?

8. Despite living in a fairly nice neighborhood, and Ethel being such a good role model, her teenage great-granddaughter Cynthia had some attitude problems. Because she had to follow Ethel's rules, she felt picked on, so she ran away from home on a regular basis. Do you think Ethel's spending most of her time away from their apartment working and giving

Cynthia a lot of household responsibilities caused Cynthia's woeful angst? Or was she only being a typical teenager, like Rosemary suggested?

9. What did you think of the water-in-the-glass demonstration Rosemary performed for Cynthia? Do you think it is a good example to show a rebellious teenager?

10. When Cynthia found out Ethel was moving their family in with Eugene and Rosemary, she didn't just run away again. Instead she moved in with her best friend's family so she could stay in the same neighborhood. She was flabbergasted when she found out the kids in that family also had rules to follow and specific responsibilities, and that the same ones would apply to her. When Cynthia realized she'd have the same "problems" with adults telling her what to do, no matter where she lived, she looked at things from a different perspective. Were you surprised when she showed up at Eugene and Rosemary's house on Christmas Day, hoping they still wanted her to be part of their family?

11. Within six months of living with Eugene and Rosemary, Cynthia's attitude changed dramat-

ically for the better. Do you think that if Ethel had not moved them in with Eugene and Rosemary, Cynthia's behavior would have gotten worse?

12. Ethel felt that she'd been so blessed and lived such a long, productive life, she didn't want a traditional funeral. She wanted people to "celebrate" her death, not mourn. How do you want people to honor you when you pass?

13. Do you think Ethel's passing was the best way to end this story? Explain why you think so, or why you don't think so?